ASHES TO ASHES

MINISTRY OF CURIOSITIES, BOOK #5

C.J. ARCHER

WWW.CJARCHER.COM

CHAPTER 1

LONDON, WINTER 1889

*I*f anyone had been in Grand View Lane on that freezing December night, for a mere moment they would have seen a shadowy figure hanging from the garret window at the back of the derelict house, before dropping to the second floor window ledge. With the agility of a monkey, the black-clad figure repeated the exercise to reach the window ledge on the first floor, and finally landed silently on the greasy cobblestones below. The phantom-like figure wore no cloak or coat to hinder his movement, and his black shoulder-length hair was tied with a ribbon at his nape. There were no witnesses to this feat, however, and that was the way Lincoln Fitzroy preferred it.

Despite its name, Grand View Lane wasn't grand, and the only views it offered during the day were of damp brick walls and an empty cart with a broken axle, leaning drunkenly against the low wall at the end of the lane. It was difficult to see in the dark, but Lincoln had memorized its position and could make out its shape well enough. There was nobody else about. It was too cold, too dark, and too dangerous to be out in the middle of the night in a part of London that the Ripper had made infamous a year before.

He melted into the shadows and waited. He'd purposefully come an hour earlier than the arranged time. That way he could see if an accomplice entered the lane and hid ahead of Lincoln's informant. Lincoln wasn't taking any chances.

The fog crept in like a slow moving spirit. That's how Charlie had described ghosts to him—misty clouds that formed the shape of their living selves.

Charlie. She would be asleep now, tucked into a warm bed at the School for Wayward Girls many miles away. Safe.

He shoved thoughts of her aside before they took root and became too stubborn to remove. He had to concentrate.

The fog dampened the already frigid air. He breathed through his nose into his upturned jacket collar, to hide his frosty breath, and curled his gloved fingers into fists to keep the tips warm. He shivered and silently cursed the bitter weather. It wasn't lost on him that he never used to feel the cold. He never used to feel anything.

Once again he had to force himself to concentrate. He listened. Mary Dwyer, the prostitute who occupied the garret room he'd just come from, must have found a client. Her over-enthusiastic gasps almost drowned out the drunkard singing in the adjoining street. Lincoln should pay her more next time he needed to use her room as an entrance to the lane. It was too easy for someone to pretend to be a customer but instead use the room as Lincoln had done and attack from above. An hour of her time should suffice.

The singing drew closer, clearer. It wasn't slurred enough for a drunkard. If anyone had been listening as intently as Lincoln, they would have noticed. The singer entered the lane without pausing and his singing stopped altogether. Lincoln rolled his eyes. If his men had dropped their disguises so quickly, he'd have made them do extra work around the house and more training. They hadn't made such an amateurish mistake in weeks.

The informant disturbed the fog, parting it like a sea, only to have it settle behind him again once the flap of his cloak subsided. He wore a cap pulled low to cover his face and didn't lift the brim, even when he stopped near the cart. His breaths were loud in the silence and formed clouds at his mouth.

"You here?" he whispered.

Lincoln waited without speaking or moving. He reached out with his seer's senses but felt no other presence. It wasn't all that reliable. So he listened, too. There were no other sounds. Mary Dwyer had finished and would go in search of another customer soon. She might even catch the singer on his way out, if he was the sort to be tempted by cheap, yellow-haired, toothless hags. Lincoln didn't know. He knew as much about the man as he needed to know, including the fact he went by the name Billy the Bolter. His usual informant had set up the meeting, after telling Lincoln that Billy claimed to have overheard a conversation where one man offered another a large sum of money to kill a third. If there was any chance that Billy could identify the procurer, Lincoln would do whatever it took to get that information out of him, even if it required patience rather than force. He suspected money would suffice, however. Money was easy to give away, and fortunately most criminals spilled their knowledge as soon as Lincoln flashed a few coins. He'd give Billy the Bolter an entire sack full, if it led to the fellow who'd hired the assassin who'd shot dead two supernaturals, Reginald Drinkwater and Joan Brumley. It was that man Lincoln wanted to find before he located more supernaturals to kill.

Before he located Charlie.

Lincoln might not want to be anywhere near her himself,

but he felt physically ill when he thought of anyone harming her. He tightened his fist at his side, then said, "I'm here."

Billy the Bolter whipped around. He peered into the shadows near the cart. "Where? Come out so's I can see you."

"No."

Billy was silent, perhaps trying to decide if he could do business with a man who hid in shadows. "You got the chink?"

Lincoln removed a pouch from his inside jacket pocket and held it out. He didn't want to toss it. The coins would make too much noise.

Billy jerked as if surprised to know that Lincoln stood so close. He took the pouch and weighed it in his palm. "It ain't enough."

"You'll get the other half after our conversation."

"Afraid I'll bolt with yer ready, eh?" Billy laughed. Lincoln waited. "They call me Billy the Bolter, see. Bolter. Bolt. It's a pun."

Lincoln didn't move.

Billy sighed. "Jim said you was as much o' a lark as a plank o' wood." After a brief pause, in which the only sound came from Billy's throat as he swallowed, the informant finally got to the point. "Jim said you want to know about that cove who's been lookin' for a shooter."

"You were approached?"

"Nah, not me. I ain't got no barkers. Me mate, now, he's got a revolver. It were him what spoke to the toff, but I were watchin' from the next table. I saw everythin'."

"Toff? He was a gentleman?"

"Aye, real plummy accent."

"What did he look like?"

"Tall, red hair, gray beard, fat, and he had on round specs. Wore a long black cloak, made of fine wool, it were."

Lincoln's heart sank. The red hair and gray beard didn't

match the descriptions he'd already gathered from his other informants. One had met a beardless man, another had described the fellow as blond and slender, yet another claimed he was young with brown hair and of average weight. The only thing they agreed on was that the man was tall. A man's height was impossible to disguise. The rest could be changed with wigs, glasses, and padding.

"What about a name?" Lincoln asked.

"Are you bleedin' stupid?"

It was worth a try. "Did he have a conveyance?"

"Black hack, no markings."

"What about the driver and horse?"

"Driver were wrapped to the eyeballs in his cloak, the horse were brown. I didn't follow him, if that's yer next question. I didn't want to make meself known to him."

"You took careful note of these things because you knew I would pay for information?"

"Aye. Jim told me."

How many people had Jim told? "Did your friend refuse the job or did the toff decide to go elsewhere after meeting him?"

Billy's pause made Lincoln frown. "How do you know he didn't take it?"

Because the killer had turned up dead a week ago, most likely silenced by the toff's hand, and Billy spoke as if his friend were still alive. "I just do."

"He refused it. He ain't no killer, see. He just uses the barker to scare folk out o' their jewels and the like."

"Why did it take you this long to approach me?" Lincoln had been speaking to informants earlier in the week, but there'd been no word from them in two days. Billy the Bolter might have delayed because he couldn't decide if lying to collect the reward was a risk worth taking. Jim would have told him what happened to informants who misled Lincoln.

Billy rocked back. "It were only last night."

"Last night?"

"God's truth! I knew you would pay because Jim told me so, but it were only last night that it happened. I spoke wiv Jim today, and he set up this meetin'."

That he had. If the exchange had only happened last night, either someone else was looking for a killer to hire, or the toff who'd commissioned the murders of the supernaturals was going to kill again.

Lincoln wasn't surprised. It had only been a matter of time. Fortunately, with Charlie gone, he could now focus on finding out who was behind the murders and stop them before they killed again.

"Is there anything else you can tell me?" Lincoln asked.

"Nope." Billy held out his hand and Lincoln placed another pouch onto it.

"There'll be more of that if you can find out anything else of note about the toff, or the gunman he hires."

"Aye, sir. I'll be all ears and eyes."

"Breathe a word about this meeting to anyone and I'll slit your throat."

"You got to catch me first." Billy danced away then turned to run.

Lincoln silently cursed the entire criminal classes for their arrogance and sprinted after him. He caught Billy well before the lane opened up onto the main street. He twisted the scum's arm behind his back and clamped a hand over his mouth. No one would have seen—Whitechapel wasn't known for its working streetlamps—but there was a chance someone had heard Billy's muffled cry of pain.

"As I was saying," Lincoln said with quiet menace, "do not tell a soul. I know where you live. I know where your family lives. No one will be harmed if you abide by my rule of silence."

Billy nodded quickly and Lincoln let him go. "H-how do you know where I live?"

The fellow was audacious to ask. "I make sure to investigate all my informants...William John Hamlin."

Billy rubbed his arm and backed away, almost tripping over his own cap, which had fallen off when Lincoln caught him. "Blimey," Billy muttered. "Jim were right about you. He said you was the devil himself, hidin' in the shadows, watchin' and waitin' for someone to wrong you. And when they do..." He sliced his finger across his throat to mimic a knife cut.

Lincoln picked up Billy's cap, careful to keep the man's feet in his line of sight. Billy didn't move, not even a shifting of his weight. It would seem he had no intention of crossing Lincoln, or he would have taken the opportunity to attack.

"You're not the first person to mistake me for the devil." He handed Billy his cap, but didn't let go immediately. "I doubt you'll be the last." It was difficult to glare at the man in the dark, but hopefully Billy heard the threatening tone and understood the implications if he tattled. Lincoln let go of the cap. "Good evening."

"Er, uh, good evenin', sir." The stutters and the "sir" were a good sign that Billy the Bolter would be complicit.

Lincoln watched as Billy backed out of the lane. When he reached the end, he fled. Lincoln didn't follow. Instead, he returned to the back of the lane, hopped into the cart, then leaped over the wall. The yard on the other side was empty, the shabby tenements surrounding it dark. He quickly scanned the area then exited through the archway and onto the street. He ran down another alley, then another so narrow that his shoulders skimmed the walls on either side.

He turned a corner and pulled up quickly as two constables approached from the other direction. Fortunately they had their heads down, bent into the breeze. If Lincoln hadn't been so distracted by his thoughts, he would have been more cautious. He came across another two constables on patrol before leaving Whitechapel altogether. The police had become more vigilant since the Ripper murders. It was too little too late for the victims.

Seth and Gus waited for him with the carriage outside Liverpool Street Station. They both nodded when they saw him but didn't speak. Gus took up his position at the back and Lincoln climbed inside the cabin without bothering to lower the step. Seth wasted no time in driving off and they were soon speeding through the poorly lit London streets to Highgate. They skirted Hampstead Heath and rolled through the iron gates of Lichfield Towers.

Lincoln spared a glance for the house as Seth drove around the side of one broad wing to the stables and coach house, although Lincoln avoided looking up at the central tower, as he always did these days. There were no lights lit in any of the dozens of windows, no smoke drifting from the many chimneys. It was grayer and grimmer than ever, like it was going into hibernation for winter. Some would call it an impressive example of Gothic architecture, a magnificent English mansion, but to Lincoln it was nothing more than a roof over his head. He would have been as satisfied living in the cellar of a burnt out building, as Charlie had done for years before coming to Lichfield.

She called the great, hulking pile of gray stone 'home'. Women were sentimental about these things, and Charlie in particular had a strong emotional streak that influenced her thoughts and actions. She'd quickly developed an attachment to Lichfield, once she settled in. He'd been warned that would happen. He should have listened.

But Charlie was gone, and he doubted the others who lived at Lichfield saw the place as she did. They were practical men. Emotion didn't rule them. They had come to live

8

there, and work for Lincoln, purely for financial gain. It was time to remind them of that, since they seemed to have forgotten it lately. Only the day before, Seth, Gus and Cook had threatened to leave. Mere months ago, none would have dared.

"What did you learn, sir?" Gus asked, as Lincoln alighted from the cabin outside the coach house. "Did he know anything?"

"Nothing useful," Lincoln said.

"Want to tell us what was said over a drink in the library? We won't be long here."

"No." Lincoln strode off. Even with his back to them, he heard the drawn-in breath of frustration from Gus, and Seth's silence was telling. Of all of them, Seth didn't hold back his opinion anymore. It was probably because he believed in his God-given right as a nobleman to rule commoners, even those who'd saved him from getting his face smashed in at an illegal bareknuckle fight and now paid his wages.

Lincoln made his way upstairs and along the corridor, determined to get all the way to his own room this time without stopping. He failed, however, and paused outside Charlie's door. No, not *her* door, anymore. He rested his hand on the doorknob but didn't twist it. After a moment, he let it go, satisfied that yet again he hadn't succumbed to the temptation to enter. He hadn't been inside since he'd tried to pack her things on the morning she'd left.

That morning was etched into his memory and couldn't be removed, no matter how hard he tried. He couldn't forget the wavering pitch of her voice as she'd questioned him, shouted at him, pleaded with him, and finally acquiesced. Nor could he forget the way her eyes changed shape and color with each emotion, and the way her expressive mouth told him what she was really thinking when her words did not. He remembered all too clearly the stab in his gut and the ache in his throat when her tear-soaked face looked up at him as he watched her departure from the tower room—the room she'd reluctantly occupied upon her arrival at Lichfield.

As with all bad memories, the best he could do was to push it to one side, where he didn't stumble over it every moment of every day. Sometimes, that even worked.

* * *

DOYLE BROUGHT IN THE NEWSPAPER, along with Lincoln's breakfast. The man was efficient, professional and unobtrusive, all qualities Lincoln liked in his staff. While Seth, Gus and Cook were reasonably efficient, they lacked the other two attributes. They had also shed most of their reserve in the last few weeks and even dared to speak to Lincoln as if he were their equal, if not their friend. Doyle still feared and respected him. Another reason to like him.

It was still dark, and Lincoln lit the lamp on his desk to spread out the newspaper. Doyle had ironed out the creases, even though Lincoln had told him it was unnecessary. He picked up his teacup, only to set it down again as he read the headline on the front page: CIRCUS STRONG MAN SHOT IN HEAD AS HE SLEPT. Lincoln scanned the article. By the end, he was sure he had another supernatural murder on his hands.

According to the article, after the show at the Olympia ended, the victim had retired to his lodgings for the evening, alone. A gunshot had woken some of the other performers around two AM. When they investigated, they found Brutus dead in his bed. No one had seen the killer leave, and the police had no suspects. The performers claimed the victim was a good man with no enemies. The article went on to describe the feats of strength Brutus displayed in his act. It was the lifting of the brougham clear off the ground that intrigued Lincoln. No man could do that. No *normal* man, not even a strong one.

But the piece of information that really gave him pause was the name. Brutus was a pseudonym used for the act. His actual name was Patrick O'Neill. Lincoln recognized it.

He dressed and headed up to the attic where the ministry archives were stored. They were copies he'd made when he'd first started working at Lichfield. The original files were kept at Julia, Lady Harcourt's Mayfair house. Lincoln had made copies not only to familiarize himself with supernaturals and their powers, but also to have the files on site where he could access them. He hadn't trusted any of the committee members to give him access back then, and he certainly didn't trust them now.

The attic had been visited a number of times recently, as the files were checked and updated after the last murders. Each of the small drawers contained approximately twenty files, some taking up several pages. Much of the information in those longer documents had been gathered centuries ago and followed descendants through the generations to the present. The originals had been written on parchment, but these copies were on ordinary paper. Many of the files were no longer active, the hereditary line having died out. There were a little over two hundred active ones, one of which was Patrick O'Neill's.

Lincoln remembered the details clearly, but he pulled out the file anyway to re-read it. According to the document, Patrick O'Neill was descended from a line of supernaturals based in Ireland. Their power wasn't strength, but moving objects with their minds. It was the same power that Reginald Drinkwater possessed. The file listed O'Neill's last known address as New York, where he'd taken up with Barnum and Bailey's circus troupe.

According to the newspaper article on his desk, the "Greatest Show on Earth" had come to London for the winter and had already performed several shows at the Olympia in Kensington. Lincoln had seen the advertisements describing the star acts, including that of Brutus himself. Was it the claim of "super-human strength" that had caught the killer's eye, or had the ministry's archive been accessed and O'Neill's name found there?

If it were the latter, the suspects narrowed considerably, and in a direction that worried Lincoln. He might not like or trust the committee members, but he hadn't pegged any of them as murderers.

Then again, the murders had been carried out by a middleman. It was easier to kill someone when you didn't pull the trigger yourself and could simply read about it in the papers the next day. It was the best way to assure anonymity, if the hired gunman's silence could be bought.

Other recent events and coincidences bothered Lincoln too, not just the murders. How had the committee known that Charlie raised the body of Estelle Pearson, for one? Spies, of course, but who had hired the spies? Lincoln had found none lurking outside the gates of Lichfield, but he hadn't checked before the event, only after, when his suspicions had been raised. Also, who had known that Charlie regularly rode Rosie and cut through the saddle straps? Perhaps that had been a guess, considering Rosie was the only small mare in the stable, and there had only been one side saddle.

Whether the committee were involved or not remained to be seen, but at least Charlie was out of the way now. Sending her north had solved that dilemma, although it hadn't been his primary reason for organizing the position at the school for her. He'd done it so he could work at his best again, without distraction or hindrance. Having her nearby played havoc with his attention. Now he could focus once more.

The fact he was thinking about her *again* wasn't lost him. But those thoughts would become fewer soon, he was sure of it. It was just a matter of time.

He returned O'Neill's file to the drawer and was met on the staircase by Doyle, who was out of breath and looked relieved to see him.

"There you are," said Seth, striding along the corridor from the right. Gus came from the left, and both converged on the staircase as if they were trying to trap their employer. "Where were you?"

Since when did his men question where he'd been? "Attic. There's been another supernatural murder."

Gus and Seth both swore, their language as colorful as it had been before Charlie arrived. The very proper Doyle didn't bat an eyelid. He pressed his hand to his chest and murmured, "Dear lord. Will you be investigating, sir?"

Lincoln had previously told Doyle that he was the leader of a secretive semi-government organization that investigated crimes the police couldn't solve. He'd left out the part about supernaturals. It explained the comings and goings at Lichfield well enough without worrying the man unnecessarily.

Lincoln nodded. "Seth and Gus, prepare the coach and horses." He strode past Seth, back to his rooms. "We're going to the circus."

CHAPTER 2

*L*incoln was rarely surprised, and never astounded, but watching the acrobats, exotic animals and other performers parade into the vast hall of the Olympia, he came close. Some performers traveled in golden chariots, others sat atop one of the thirteen elephants, or rode horses and camels, while yet others led in zebras, carried monkeys, or simply danced or tumbled. There was no strong man, of course, but the crowd whispered Brutus's name in hushed, shocked tones. If the performers missed O'Neill's presence among them, on this first show following his death, they gave no indication. Their smiles were wide and bright.

A brass band led the parade past the grandstands where Lincoln and Seth sat, along with thousands of others. Seth's jaw fell open as he watched the spectacle pass by. For a worldly individual, he could be childlike sometimes.

"There must be hundreds of people involved," Seth breathed. "My God!" He leaned forward and squinted at the large glass container passing by on the back of a horse-drawn cart. The box contained water and a woman. "Is that a mermaid?"

"No," Lincoln said. "Mermaids aren't real."

Seth sat back with a *humph*. "Spoil sport."

Lincoln refrained from retorting that Seth should know better, given his education. Clearly a good education and gullibility weren't mutually exclusive.

The menagerie split up and filled the three rings and two stages. Riders performed tricks on horseback in one ring, acrobats tumbled in another, elephants lifted their left forelegs in unison in another, while a vaudevillian show and ballet occupied the stages.

"I don't know where to look," Seth said, his gaze flicking between each of the performances.

"That's the point," Lincoln told him.

"What?"

He sounded distracted, but Lincoln explained anyway. "With so many acts on at once, it's impossible to see everything. You'll leave here today wanting to come back and see the things you missed. You'll buy another ticket for tomorrow on your way out."

"Or get one the way you did." Seth flashed him a grin, but it quickly withered and he turned back to the show.

Lincoln had been prepared to pay for tickets, but it seemed all of London wanted to see the famous Barnum and Bailey circus, and the show was sold out. Lincoln had resorted to picking the pocket of a passing gentleman.

Seth applauded along with the audience as an aerialist dressed in short pantaloons somersaulted in mid-air and caught a swinging bar high above them. "Charlie would love this." Lincoln felt Seth's gaze burning into him. "You should bring her when she comes home," he went on.

Lincoln didn't bother correcting him. It never seemed to sink in that Charlie wasn't coming back, no matter how many times Lincoln told him.

Lincoln stood and headed back down the aisle, away from

the spectacles. He didn't wait to see if Seth followed but he heard his footsteps.

"Was it something I said?" The pout in Seth's voice was as much an act as the performances in the rings.

Lincoln fisted his hand at his side. Hitting Seth wouldn't be wise when he wanted to move around the Olympia undetected. Maybe later, after they'd finished investigating, he'd offer to spar with him to relieve some tension. They both needed to get it out of their system.

They skirted the perimeter of the enormous Olympia theater. Most of the spectators were inside watching the displays, giving the sideshow freaks time to themselves, away from their booths. Nobody paid Lincoln and Seth any attention, not even when Seth gawped at the oddities.

"Did you see that girl?" he whispered. "She has two heads!"

Lincoln didn't think he warranted an answer, so he gave none.

"Blimey, that man has three legs." A moment later, Seth made a horrified sound. "I've seen some hairy women in my time, but she takes the cake. Do you think she's just a man dressed like a woman?"

"Ask her for proof."

"Do you think she'd mind?"

Lincoln's gaze slid to Seth to see if he was serious. Seth kept a straight face; it would seem he didn't realize Lincoln had made a joke.

After several moments of silence, in which he continued to stare at the circus folk, Seth finally said, "If the thin man and the fat lady had children together, do you think they would be normal, or either thin or fat?"

There was no point joking about the logistics of such an arrangement if Seth wasn't going to laugh, even though Lincoln could think of several comments that would have had Charlie smirking at the very least.

He strode on in search of the strong man's neighbor, Lionel the lion-faced man. That morning, during a brief visit to the lodging house where the victim was found dead in his room, Lincoln had overheard the landlady give the police the name of the lodger occupying the next room. There'd been too many policemen crawling through the house to take a closer look or speak to her then. Lincoln would return later that night for a more thorough investigation.

In the meantime, he could question the lion-faced man. They found him in a tent at the back of the Olympia grounds, sipping tea and chatting to another man with scaly skin on his neck and face. They were wrapped in woolen cloaks against the cold, but neither wore hats or gloves. Lionel was indeed covered with real hair growing out of his skin. It was a soft golden brown color, like that on the top of his head, and covered every inch of his face except for his eyes and mouth. A lion was an apt description.

"You speak with him," Seth whispered. "I'll wait here."

"He looks like a lion, he doesn't behave like one."

"How do you know? Have you ever met a lion-faced man before? And that other fellow looks like a lizard." Seth shivered. "It's not normal."

Lincoln stopped and rounded on his employee. "You're coming. You might be needed."

Seth took a step back. In alarm? "What for?"

"Talking." People found Seth charming. He was good at setting folk at ease, and that could be useful when questioning witnesses. On this occasion, however, Lincoln doubted Seth's charm would work when he seemed so uneasy himself.

Lincoln approached the two men. Both watched warily, but made no challenge. "Are you Lionel?" He wished the landlady had mentioned his last name, but Lionel was all Lincoln had heard.

17

Lionel nodded cautiously. "It's Ira, actually. Ira Irwin. Lionel is a stage name."

"Who're you?" the lizard-man snapped.

"We're private inquiry agents, employed by Mr. Barnum and Mr. Bailey to find O'Neill's killer," Lincoln said.

"Isn't that what the police are for?"

"The police in England aren't very efficient."

Irwin snorted. "Much like our American ones."

"So Bailey hired you, eh?" Lizard's brows lifted. Now that he was closer, Lincoln could see there weren't actual scales on the man's face but an intricate tattoo made to resemble scales. "Can't believe he'd spend money on one of us freaks."

"He wants to catch the killer and see him brought to justice."

Both Irwin and Lizard snorted. "You mean he wants to make a dollar out of it somehow," Lizard said.

The light breeze drifted through the tent opening and brushed the hair on Irwin's face like grass in a meadow. "So you want to ask me some questions?" he asked in his American drawl. "I can only tell you what I already told the police. I heard nothing before the gunshot. It woke me up and set my heart racing. Took me a few moments to figure out what it was, and when I did, I got out of bed and went to investigate. The hall was empty at first, then Mrs. Mather, the landlady, joined me, and the other circus performers lodging in her house too. When we were all assembled, we realized O'Neill wasn't with us, so we knocked on his door. There was no answer so we went inside and saw…" He wrinkled his hairy nose. "There was blood everywhere, and his face was blown off."

Lizard rested a hand on Irwin's shoulder. Both men bowed their heads.

"I keep seeing the scene in my head," Irwin went on, his

voice thin and tight. "All that blood and bits of brain everywhere. I don't envy Mrs. Mather cleaning it up."

"Did you hear any other noises, either before or immediately after?" Lincoln asked.

"Like I said, I was asleep before. After, maybe I heard some footsteps running off, but I can't be sure. I was still trying to figure out what had woken me."

"Did O'Neill have any enemies within the circus?" Seth asked. "Anyone who might want to harm him?"

"No!" Lizard cried. "We're like family, even the non-freaks."

"He wasn't a freak?"

"He was normal, just like you, only he was real strong."

"Was there any trickery to his feats of strength?" Lincoln asked. "Hidden wires and pulleys?"

"No," Irwin said, sounding offended. "He was as real as I am." He grabbed a fistful of hair on his forehead and tugged. It didn't come away.

Seth's swallow was audible. "We believe you," he said quickly. "Just trying to establish facts. So you can't think of anyone he wronged?"

"No," Lizard said, as Irwin shook his head.

"What about women?" Lincoln asked.

"What about them?" Irwin said.

"Did any go to his room?"

"On occasion." He glanced at Lizard.

Lizard nodded. "Go on. If it'll help find who did this, tell him."

"He would meet up with one of the dancers sometimes," Irwin said. "I could hear them through the wall."

"Her name?"

"I don't know. She's a Polak, I think."

"Ela," Lizard said.

"How do you know?"

Lizard winked at his friend. "I asked her."

Irwin blinked. "Oh. Of course."

"She's very beautiful," Lizard went on. "She's got hair like midnight and skin like milk. If you wait for the dancers to finish the show, you'll see her. She's the prettiest and has the best figure." His tongue darted out and licked his lower lip. Lincoln wondered if he knew it made him even more lizard-like. Perhaps that was why he did it.

"Thank you." Lincoln walked out of the tent.

A moment later, Seth caught up to him. "That was interesting," he said. When Lincoln didn't respond, he elaborated. "Perhaps the killer didn't kill the strong man because of his supernatural ability. Perhaps it was Irwin. Did you notice the way he spoke about the dancer? I'd wager he was in love with her, but she shunned him for the better looking man. When Irwin saw her with O'Neill, he killed him out of jealousy."

Lincoln shook his head. "His account of last night wasn't fabricated.

"How do you know?"

"I just do." Lincoln's psychic senses may not be very strong, but he could sometimes tell when he was being lied to, although not always. Irwin was what Lincoln called "readable." The man hadn't lied.

Still, Seth might be right. The strong man's death could have nothing to do with his supernatural power. It shouldn't be too difficult to find out if anyone wished to kill him out of jealousy.

"Are we going to find Ela the dancer?" Seth asked, keeping pace.

"Yes."

"Good."

Lincoln rolled his eyes but Seth was looking forward and wouldn't have seen.

They made their way back to the main building, where

two men stood guard at the rear doors, ordering curious onlookers to move on. Applause filtered out from inside, and the band struck up a bold, brassy tune.

"You take the smaller one," Lincoln told Seth.

Seth caught his jacket sleeve. Lincoln glared at him until he let go. "Are you mad?" Seth hissed. "It's broad daylight! We'll be spotted."

"Pull your hat brim lower."

"That's it? That's your suggested disguise?"

Lincoln adjusted his hat and pulled up his coat collar.

He left Seth and wandered over to the burlier of the two guards. The man's thick neck bulged over his collar and his eyes almost disappeared into the surrounding fat.

"This is a restricted area," the man said. "Move along."

With a small twist of his arm, Lincoln dropped the knife he kept tucked up his sleeve into his palm. He showed it to the guard. "*You* move, or I will kill you."

Seth had decided to join in, and snuck up behind the other fellow. He must have shoved the point of his knife into the man's back because he lurched forward. "No harm will come to you if you move now," Seth said to his man. "If you don't, there'll be chaos, and I don't think your bosses will appreciate the bad publicity."

The two men exchanged glances, but neither moved. They didn't look particularly bright. The stupid ones usually needed decisions to be made for them. Lincoln thrust the blade forward, causing the big fellow to spring back on surprisingly nimble feet and swear loudly.

Lincoln dodged to his right and, when the guard moved to catch him, changed direction and slipped in behind him. He thrust the knife into the man's back as Seth had done to his opponent. It wasn't lost on Lincoln that his employee had chosen a better approach than he had. He pushed harder, digging through the layers of clothing to skin. The music drew closer. There was no time for delay.

"To the wagon," he said, hustling the guard toward a small, crimson wagon with gold lions, mermaids and tigers painted on the side. Lincoln recognized it from the parade. "Get inside."

"We just want to talk to one of the girls," Seth told them as he hustled his guard forward too. "No harm will come to her or anyone else."

"Then why not just pass us some ready?" his guard said. "We arrange meetings between the girls and toffs all the time."

"Is that so?" Seth growled, no doubt for Lincoln's benefit. "How much?"

"For you, two quid each."

"That's bloody robbery! We only want to talk."

"That's what they all say."

"One," Lincoln said. "Or we do this our way." He let his fellow go, but remained sprung, ready to attack.

The man simply held out his palm. When Lincoln didn't move, Seth paid him.

All four returned to the doors. A group of children approached, excited grins on their faces. "Git lost," the thick-necked guard snarled at them. "You ain't allowed back here."

"We only want to look," said a sandy-haired boy with freckles.

"I said, git lost!" The guard raised his hand, but Lincoln caught it.

The children scampered away and Lincoln let go.

"I weren't going to hit him," the guard mumbled. "Just give him a scare."

The doors opened and performers spilled into the wintry sunshine. Further along, the animals and their handlers used an unguarded exit.

"Do you know Ela the dancer?" Lincoln asked the guard.

The fellow's gaze narrowed. "You a lord?"

"No."

"Rich?"

Lincoln merely looked at him.

The guard's top lip curled up. "You ain't got no chance with Ela if you ain't a lord or rich."

"That's not what I hear."

"Or a strong man," the guard added, with a chuckle that made the flesh of his neck shake like jelly.

Lincoln watched the procession of acrobats dressed in white tights and red costumes, cut low at the bust and high up the thighs like Elizabethan trunk hose.

"Does Ela have regular liaisons with any of the other performers?" Lincoln asked the guard.

"Why do you want to know?"

"We're private inquiry agents, looking into the death of Patrick O'Neill. The police here in England are useless, and your employers want to find the killer." If the story had worked once, it should work again.

It did. The guard nodded his approval. "Good. Glad they're doing something right by the acts for once." He stroked his heavy jaw. "She weren't with anyone else that I knew, just the strongman. Of course, there were others outside the circus."

"Lords or rich men?"

"Both."

"Do you have any names?"

"No." His hand whipped out and he grabbed the arm of one of the girls walking past—a pretty dark-haired girl with a tiny waist and large bosom that was barely covered by the flimsy outfit. "Gentleman here wants to speak with you, Ela."

Ela told the other dancers that she would meet them later,

after she found out if "this one" was "worth it." She spoke in her native Polish, a language Lincoln was familiar with.

She turned a bright smile onto him. It became even brighter when Seth joined them. "*Two* handsome gentlemen?" she said in a thick accent. "I am lucky girl."

"We want to speak with you," Lincoln said.

Seth held up his hand for silence. Lincoln clamped his teeth together. "My dear," Seth said, turning on his smile. "It's Ela, isn't it?"

She nodded. "And you are?"

"Lord Vickers." He removed his hat and swept into a low bow.

The girl held out her hand and Seth kissed it. "I am pleased to meet you, Lord Vickers. Did you and your friend enjoy our performance?"

"Very much. You danced beautifully. So graceful! So elegant!"

"Thank you. You are very kind." She placed a hand on her hip and lowered her heavily made-up eyelids. The coquettish move made Seth stand straighter.

"We have some questions for you regarding the death of Mr. O'Neill," Lincoln said.

Everything about her suddenly changed, from her assured stance to the color of her face. It was as if her life force drained out of her. Her lower lip wobbled and she bit it. If it was an act, Lincoln couldn't detect the lie.

With a jerk of her head, she led them away from the eavesdroppers. "Why are you asking questions about Patrick?"

Lincoln repeated his story. "Did he have any enemies within the circus?"

She shook her head. "Everyone like Patrick. He was kind, good."

"Was he your only lover here?"

Seth shook his head and muttered something Lincoln couldn't hear. Lincoln ignored him.

Ela gasped and placed a hand to her bosom. "I find your question very rude, sir."

"Just answer it. Please."

Her lips flattened. "I have no other circus lover, only him. I know why you are asking this, and I think you are wrong. No one in the circus would kill Patrick. No one. We are like family."

"What about someone from outside the circus? Did any of your English gentlemen friends resent that you had another lover?"

She folded her arms beneath her bosom, pushing them up. Seth shifted his stance. "No one outside circus knew about Patrick and me," Ela said.

"Are you sure?"

"I cannot be certain, no." She studied her painted fingernails, and Lincoln waited for her to continue. She had something further to say, he was sure of it. "There is one man who is, how you say? Persist?"

"Persistent," Seth said.

"Yes, persistent. He demands to see me every night after the second show, and wishes for me to stay with him in his house until morning. But I cannot. I need to sleep, and Mr. Bailey would be very angry if he found out. So would Patrick, if he knew," she added with a quiet sigh. "Poor Patrick."

"Did you love him?" Seth asked.

"Bah! Love is for rich girls, not poor. I like Patrick, but he is—was—a circus man, and I do not want to be in circus my whole life."

"Would your persistent gentleman friend have saved you from this life?"

"No. He was a lord, or lord's son. I am not for marrying,

so he tell me. He only wed English girl." She swore in Polish. There was no equivalent in English, but it wasn't a word Lincoln associated with delicate dancers.

"Do you think he knew about your relationship with O'Neill?" Lincoln asked.

"No. I tell him he is only one. That is best way."

That didn't mean he hadn't found out. "This man's name?"

She bit her lip and it took some gentle coaxing from Seth to get her to talk again. "Andrew. Andrew Buchanan."

CHAPTER 3

$\mathcal{N}$either Andrew Buchanan nor his stepmother, Julia, were at Harcourt House, so Lincoln instructed Gus to drive on to Lichfield. Upon entering the long, sweeping drive, it became clear why no one was at home at Harcourt House—Julia's carriage stood behind the conveyances of Lords Gillingham and Marchbank, and General Eastbrooke.

"Want me to turn about, sir?" Gus shouted over the rumble of wheels.

"Drive on," Lincoln said. He had to face the committee members sooner or later. It was surprising that he hadn't seen them for some time—since before Charlie left. Breaking the news to them about her departure would be…interesting.

Gus stopped alongside the other carriages so that Lincoln could enter via the front door, something he rarely did. Doyle met him and informed him that the visitors were waiting in the newly refurbished drawing room upstairs, rather than the smaller downstairs parlor.

"They insisted on staying, sir." Doyle kept his voice low as he took Lincoln's coat and gloves.

"Bring tea," Lincoln said.

"Tea has been served, sir."

Lincoln made his way up to the drawing room. He'd been in it only once since the new furniture arrived from France. He'd been avoiding the room. The new pieces had been chosen by Charlie during their recent Parisian sojourn, and he saw her touch in everything. At least this time he would be distracted by the committee members and their inevitable barrage of questions.

"Finally!" Gillingham grumbled. "We've been waiting an age for you."

"It hasn't been that long, Gilly," the general chided. He greeted Lincoln with a curt nod.

Lincoln responded with a nod of his own. It was the same manner in which they'd greeted one another since Lincoln could remember.

Lord Marchbank sat beside Julia on the sofa, furthest from the crackling fire. His greeting was a bland, "Afternoon, Fitzroy." Of all the committee members, he was the one Lincoln respected. There was no guile in him, no false flattery or hidden agenda. He made sound, succinct comments when he had something to say and kept to himself when he did not. He was gruff, honest, and appreciated those who were honest in return.

Julia was his opposite in every way. From her perfectly coifed hair to her shiny black boots, she was every inch a lady. She wore pearl drop earrings today and a matching pearl necklace that she'd looped around her slender white throat three times. There were more rings on her fingers than the queen's, and a pearl and jet butterfly brooch took up most of her jacket lapel. The effect was too much for daywear. While he was far from being an expert on the nature of women, he knew a little about behaviors in the animal kingdom. Her elaborate display was perhaps an attempt to catch his eye, or to outshine the woman she saw as her rival.

The woman who was conspicuous by her absence.

"Is Charlie not with you?" Julia asked, peering past him to the door.

He braced himself. "She's gone."

Julia's breath hitched. Her eyes widened ever so slightly as she once again peered past Lincoln, as if she expected him to be joking.

"Gone?" Both Marchbank and Eastbrooke repeated.

"What do you mean, gone?" Gillingham said. "Gone where?"

"She no longer lives here." Lincoln settled on a chair by the window, where it was coldest. The drawing room was larger than the parlor, and not even the blazing fire warmed the entire room. It was the first time he'd spent more than a few moments in it, and already he disliked it. He couldn't put his finger on why.

"Where is she now?" Eastbrooke asked.

"That is not your affair," Lincoln said.

As he suspected, Gillingham's protest was the loudest and involved a spray of spittle. "It most certainly is! We are the committee. It's our right to know everything that goes on in the ministry, including the location of the most dangerous supernatural."

Lincoln didn't bother responding. If he walked out now, would they pursue him? Probably.

"Agreed," the general said, pushing to his feet in a show of superiority. He had always liked to display his physical strength in one way or another. He could no longer beat Lincoln, or order anyone to beat him, but it had never stopped the general from trying to manage him. The man hadn't realized that he couldn't control Lincoln—or the other committee members—anymore. It would come as a rude shock one day.

"Why won't you tell us?" Julia asked, all innocence. "We're as invested in her safety as you are."

He knew her well enough to know when she was lying. Did the others detect it, or was he more in tune with her because he'd made the mistake of being intimate with her?

"Is she in London?" Gillingham asked when Lincoln still didn't answer.

"She is not at Lichfield. That's all you need to know."

Gillingham smashed the end of his walking stick into the floor. "Damn it, man! We must be informed."

"No, you must not."

Gillingham swore, completely disregarding Julia's presence. Not that she seemed to notice or care. She'd probably heard worse. She'd certainly said worse. She had quite a filthy tongue when she shed her noble façade.

Eastbrooke sat again with a loud click of his tongue, but he didn't protest or ask for more information. Of all of them, he knew how useless it was to swear at Lincoln or cajole, beg, or trick him into capitulating once he'd made up his mind about something. When Lincoln was a child, his stubbornness had earned him punishments that ranged from insults, isolation, and finally physical violence, mostly from his tutors but sometimes from the general himself, when he returned home from his military campaigns. Even after Lincoln grew strong enough to fight back, and his skills surpassed even those of his tutors, the general would still try to "knock some sense" into him, one way or another. He finally ceased trying to break Lincoln's stubbornness after Lincoln killed Gurry, one of his tutors.

"Keep your secret, if you like," Marchbank said. "I'm simply glad you came to your senses, finally."

The other three turned to him, once again protesting at

being left out of the decision making process. Lincoln wondered which of them really wanted to know where he'd sent Charlie, and which simply resented him overruling their authority.

It was Julia who finally called for calm. Nobody spoke as she poured tea into a cup, got up and handed it to Lincoln. The perfect hostess. Except it wasn't her place to act as mistress of the house.

Lincoln considered refusing the cup, but decided that would be petty.

"Did you send her away, or did she go of her own accord?" she asked.

"That is irrelevant." Charlie was gone, and that was that.

She blew out a frustrated breath. "There is no need for this secrecy. We're satisfied that she's gone. It's what we all wanted."

He did not remind her that at least one member would have preferred Charlie be eliminated altogether. He eyed Gillingham over the rim of his teacup as he sipped. The coward flushed and looked away.

Julia returned to the sofa and perched on the edge, her hands placed in her lap, the picture of a well brought up lady. Few knew that a snake lurked beneath that respectable, poised exterior. Lincoln knew better than anyone. What he didn't know was how much of her waspishness stemmed from her jealousy over Charlie, and how much was innate. Each private discussion between him and Julia since Charlie's arrival had become more and more uncomfortable, as she'd allowed her mask of pleasantness and respectability to slip. She'd thrown herself at him, begged him, threatened him, and once, tried to claw at his face, all because he refused to resume their liaison. Finally, shortly before he and Charlie had left for Paris, she had calmly pointed out every reason why he should send her away. None of those reasons were ones he hadn't already considered. No doubt Julia would see Charlie's banishment as a victory.

He tapped the side of his cup and counted the ripples on the tea's surface. After a moment, his temper had dampened enough that he could discuss recent events. "I assume you are here because of the death reported in this morning's papers," he said. At their nods, he added, "I've already begun my investigation. It's unclear whether this death is linked to those of Drinkwater and Brumley—"

"Of course it is," Gillingham bit off. "It must be."

"Why?"

"He could move objects with his mind, like Drinkwater. Couldn't he?"

"He could." Lincoln glared at Gillingham, hoping to get him to say more than he wanted to. Of all the committee members, he was the easiest to intimidate. "How do you know?"

Gillingham snorted. "I read about his superior strength in the article reporting on his death in this morning's papers. Nobody is that strong."

"With Drinkwater fresh in our minds," the general said, "is it surprising that we immediately thought O'Neill was a supernatural? I too was skeptical about his feats of strength."

"I recognized his name from the archives," Julia said. "After checking, I sent word to everyone to meet here this afternoon to discuss it with you."

O'Neill was hardly a memorable name, but he didn't question her. "As I said, I have already begun investigating."

"And?" the general prompted.

"And there is nothing to report yet."

Gillingham clicked his tongue. "Come on, man, we are not the enemy! You must tell us what you know."

"I will," Lincoln said through a tight jaw, "once I've learned something."

Eastbrooke held up his hands. "Very well, very well. We'll leave it with you. No, Gilly," he said when Gillingham protested. "He has never failed to keep us informed of ministry business."

"The necromancer is ministry business, and he has failed to keep us informed of her whereabouts." Gillingham stamped his stick into the floor again and pushed himself to his feet. "Good day, gentlemen, Julia."

"I'm going too," Marchbank announced, standing.

They departed, along with Eastbrooke, but Julia remained. It would probably be rude of him to ask her to leave.

"You look very tired, Lincoln," she said, frowning. "Is something troubling you?"

"No," he lied.

"I'm glad to hear it." She smiled. "I'm sure that many of your troubles have disappeared now." She came to where he sat, her steps slow and light, as if she glided across the floor. She rested a hand on his shoulder. "Perhaps you're tired because you're not sleeping well."

"That is generally the cause of tiredness."

Her hand moved from his shoulder to his neck. Her fingers skimmed his hairline. She leaned down so that the swell of her breasts brushed his cheek. "Perhaps you're not sleeping well because you're frustrated," she whispered. "I have a special remedy for frustration. A remedy that you once desired very much."

Her misguided confidence in her own appeal would have been laughable if it weren't so pathetic. How had he ever thought her alluring? She repulsed him now.

She touched his tie to loosen it, but he caught her hand. "I no longer desire your particular remedy. Good day, Julia."

She hopped off the chair arm and stepped back. Tears

welled in her eyes, as if his words had stung, but he couldn't be sure if they were real tears or false.

"She's gone, Lincoln." Her usually lilting voice turned ugly. "Your little *affaire de coeur* is over."

He finished his tea as slowly and deliberately as he could. He counted the seconds in his head.

"Whether you sent her away or she left of her own accord doesn't matter. She's gone, and it's for the best. You'll miss her for a few weeks, but it will pass and you will once again be as you were."

A few weeks. He wanted to ask if she could be more specific, but didn't. She might not even be telling the truth. As far as he was aware, she'd never been in—

He dropped the cup back in its saucer and tossed them both onto the table beside him. It clattered and possibly chipped, but he didn't care. "That's enough, Julia. It's time you left."

She pressed her hand to her heaving breast. "I—I need to speak with you about something else first. Something of a personal nature."

"More personal than what we've already been discussing?"

She blinked. "Yes." She crossed to the double doors and shut them. "I want you to speak to Mr. Golightly on my behalf."

Lincoln righted the cup and placed it in the saucer. The rim was indeed chipped. "The stage manager at The Alhambra? Why?"

She drew in a deep breath and let it out again. "I had an arrangement with him after I severed my connection to The Al before my marriage. He agreed to ensure that no one in his employ would publicly connect Lady Harcourt with Miss D.D. the dancer. After Merry Drinkwater's recent threats to expose me, I've become concerned that he isn't keeping up his end of our bargain."

"He can't control what people say once they leave his employ."

"He should try!" Her voice rose, along with her bosom as she heaved in another breath. "Oh, Lincoln, she almost exposed me."

"Almost, but not quite. How fortunate that you came up with an arrangement to satisfy her and keep her quiet." That arrangement being the kidnapping of Charlie and Gus so that Charlie could raise Mrs. Drinkwater's dead supernatural husband. Those dark hours when Lincoln hadn't known where Charlie was still ate at him. He had never known real fear until the moment when he learned that she'd been taken, perhaps killed. He never wanted to experience it again. It was after he'd learned of Julia's involvement that he'd begun to see her for the selfish woman she truly was. It had taken every ounce of his control not to kill her. The irony wasn't lost on him that he wouldn't have had that self-control if it weren't for Charlie believing he had it in him.

"Please, Lincoln." She placed her palms on his chest, tilted her chin and blinked watery eyes at him. "Please speak with Golightly and get his assurance that nothing like that will happen again."

He plucked off her hands then let them go. "That is your affair, not mine. Speak to Golightly yourself."

"But I'll be seen!"

"Then write him a letter."

"So he or that horrid Redding woman can keep it and use it against me?" She bit her wobbling lip, and this time he believed that her tears were real. "She never did like me, the jealous minx. Not once Andrew and I...not after he began paying me attention."

He passed her his handkerchief. "Speaking of Buchanan, do you know about your stepson's latest interest?"

She paused, perhaps needing a moment to adjust to the change in topic. "Interest?"

"Her name is Ela."

She swallowed. "Oh. That sort of interest. No, I didn't know about her." She lifted her chin, stretching her throat above the high lace ruffle of her collar. "Who is she?"

"A dancer with the circus."

Her bark of laughter held no humor. "Of course she is."

"You haven't seen her at Harcourt House?"

"God, no! No gentleman brings home his mistress for the world, and the servants, to see. That's obscene."

She should know, having been a gentleman's mistress prior to her marriage. Lincoln wasn't sure how she'd convinced Lord Harcourt, Andrew's father, to marry her, and he didn't want to know. The agreement struck up with Golightly had probably helped her cause considerably. Harcourt had been a respected, conservative nobleman—he wouldn't want the world thinking he'd fallen for a dancer. The fact that Julia was a headmaster's daughter had been enough of a scandal at the time.

"They must have hired a room somewhere for the purpose." She strode away, her deep plum skirts swishing around her ankles. She trailed her fingers along the back of the sofa then turned to face him, her back to the fire. Her eyes seemed to glisten, but whether from unshed tears or something else, he couldn't be sure. "Did you mention this Ela woman merely to see my reaction, Lincoln? Are you curious to know if I'm jealous of her?"

Lincoln knew that Julia and Andrew had a dalliance before she met Andrew's father. He wasn't as sure whether their affair had continued after Lord Harcourt's death, although it wouldn't surprise him if they had an arrangement. It would be easy enough, since they lived in the same house and both had passionate natures that neither seemed

36

fully able to control. But there was a tension between them with a sharp, cruel edge to it. Lincoln didn't know the source of the tension, nor did he understand why they stayed together in the same house if they didn't like one another. Their relationship, like many, was a mystery to him.

He blamed his lack of understanding on a deficiency in his education. He'd been taught a broad range of subjects, but his lack of interaction with other people meant he felt like he was always observing through a window, unable to hear the conversation on the other side.

Charlie had been good at understanding people. Years of living with gangs on the street had honed senses Lincoln doubted he even possessed. She could quickly identify subtle changes in the mood of others and the meaning behind facial expressions and tone of voice. She knew how to express her feelings, and how to coax the best out of people. And sometimes the worst.

"Lincoln? Are you listening to me?'

He snapped his gaze back to Julia. "Buchanan is your stepson," he said. "Why would you be jealous of his latest paramour?" It wasn't the cleverest thing he'd said all day, and the stiffening of her spine cued him into her opinion of it.

She sniffed. "Paramour is not quite the appropriate word, in this case. I prefer to use whore."

"She was also O'Neill's lover," he told her.

"Ah. That explains your questions. And here I thought it was to goad me."

"I don't goad."

Her lips flattened. "I'm sure the dancer is merely a passing infatuation for Andrew, but please, ask him yourself. I'm sure he would love to answer your questions."

Unlikely.

"Do you know how long the circus is in London?" she asked.

"Until February, I believe."

"That long?" She turned her back to him and held her hands out to the fire. A few deep breaths later, she turned once again and plastered a smile on her face. "I'm holding a Christmas ball soon. I'd like you to come."

"I'm too busy."

"I haven't told you which night. Besides, everyone will be there."

She'd said something similar when she wanted him to attend another ball three months prior. In that instance, she'd used the carrot of the Prince of Wales's presence. Lincoln had gone only to see the man who'd fathered him. It was the first time he had been in the same room as the prince, and it would hopefully be the last. He wanted nothing more to do with him.

Julia approached and took his hands in hers. "I'll send you an invitation. Now, what does a woman need to do to get an invitation to dinner at Lichfield?"

"I rarely dine at an appropriate hour for company."

"You're home now. We could pass the time in here or… elsewhere until the gong."

"I have work to do."

She pouted. "Don't be difficult, Lincoln." She stroked his jaw, and once again he had to catch her hand.

"Good day, Julia." He tugged the bell pull beside the door. Doyle must have been hovering nearby, because he appeared mere seconds later. "See Lady Harcourt out," Lincoln said.

Julia swept past him. He didn't need anyone to interpret her facial expression for him this time. The set of her jaw and diamond-hard stare gave him enough clues. That and her silence.

* * *

Patrick O'Neill must have been a valued member of Barnum and Bailey's troupe to get his own private room in Mrs. Mather's lodging house. Other bedrooms housed two, three or four lodgers, sometimes sharing the same bed. Lincoln had peered into each room to ascertain the layout of the house before returning to O'Neill's to begin his search.

Although he hadn't been inside the house the day before, he had been close enough to overhear the detective inspector speaking with Mrs. Mather, and he had seen their faces as they both gazed up at the third window from the right on the second story. It had been easy to use window ledges and shutter corners to scale the wall, but he would have found another way in if the relevant window had been closed. Fortunately it was open, most likely to let fresh air into a room where the scent of death still lingered beneath the equally pungent smell of carbolic soap.

The room itself was little wider than the bed. A small table had been wedged between the bed and wall, a candle burned almost to a stub on the surface. There were no lamps or other lighting. Not that Lincoln would use them if they were available. The moonlight filtering through the window was enough. That and instinct.

The mattress had been removed, along with the linen, but dark patches of what he supposed were bloodstains could still be seen splattered over the floral wallpaper behind the bed.

Lincoln worked quickly, first checking the two drawers in the dressing table. They held O'Neill's personal items—comb and hair oil, beard trimmer, a bible, rosary, ink, pen, blotter and paper. Four letters written on thin paper were tucked into the corner, all dated after the troupe's arrival in London, and all from family members still living in Ireland. Lincoln recognized their names from the ministry archives. He skimmed the contents as best as he could, given the poor light, and skimmed his fingertips over the blank papers, feeling for indentations made from the pen on the sheet that had been above it. Nothing of use. He flipped through the pages of the Bible, but nothing fell out.

He moved to the traveling trunk stored at the foot of the bed. The lock had been forced open, most likely by the police looking for clues. Moonlight glinted off the gold paint of a wide belt attached to a costume that would have covered very little of O'Neill's body. The idea was probably to show off the man's musculature, and perhaps to titillate the female audience. There were other costumes too, one Arabic in nature with pantaloons, and a loincloth made of animal hide. The trunk also contained a shirt, heavy woolen coat, a pair of trousers and old boots. His best suit and shoes must be with the body for burial. If he'd been wearing a nightshirt at the time of death, it had probably found its way to the scrap heap. Aside from a book of Irish ballads, the trunk was empty.

Lincoln searched through pockets. He flipped through the pages of the book. He searched everywhere and found exactly what he expected to find—nothing. No evidence of an argument or an enemy, gambling debts, jealous lover or grudges held. It appeared as if O'Neill's death had been a random attack.

Someone in the next room—Ira Irwin, most likely—snored. Lincoln had time to go through everything again. He searched the walls and floorboards, stepping on a creaking one near the door. He silently cursed himself for the foolish mistake then listened. All seemed quiet. Too quiet. Irwin had stopped snoring.

Lincoln hurriedly re-checked the letters, books and papers, then moved back to the clothing. Outside in the corridor, a light footstep made him pause. Someone was there. He should leave.

But he also needed to be sure he hadn't missed anything. He quickly searched through the pockets again, but they were indeed empty, and the linings contained nothing sewn into them.

He glanced at the door as another footstep sounded, so light that he questioned whether he'd heard it or imagined it. A wise man would escape now. Lincoln was in no mood to be wise tonight, or any of these last few nights. Besides, there were only O'Neill's boots remaining. He needed mere seconds.

He loosened the bootlaces and thrust his hand inside, stretching his fingers down into the toes of one boot, then the other.

Paper crinkled. He pulled it out, stood and dove for the open window, just as the door crashed back on its hinges.

"I can't see!" someone shouted.

"A figure! There! Climbing through the window!" That was Irwin. "Head him off downstairs."

Lincoln held onto the window ledge and swung to his left. He caught the ledge of Irwin's window and pulled himself up. He'd had more time to find footholds on his earlier ascent to O'Neill's room, but fortunately the layout of the building was the same here and he didn't have to think too much. As he reached the fourth level, the ceiling height was lower, the roofline sloped, and it was easy to reach the eaves.

Unfortunately, he wasn't fast enough.

"He's gone up!" Irwin shouted.

Lincoln gripped the eaves and swung, hand over hand, to the next building. Its roof was lower and Lincoln climbed onto the tiles as quietly as he could. He crossed the gully to the back of the house but the wall was too sheer to climb down. He ran up the steep, slippery pitch and glanced back toward the lodging house.

Someone had the courage to pursue him. Someone fast and unafraid of heights. An aerialist, perhaps.

Lincoln ran on. He jumped from roof to roof, leaping over narrow lanes where necessary. But he couldn't continue forever. The roofs would come to an end soon, and the aerialist hadn't given up. Lincoln could overpower him if necessary, but he didn't want to harm an innocent man.

He reached the last roof and balanced on the sloping tiles. He peered over the edge. No shutters, and the window ledges were too far apart. He ran to the back of the house and spotted a sluice pipe running down the wall. There was no time to test its strength. He swung his legs over the eaves and grabbed on with his knees.

His descent was so fast that he reached the cobbled yard before the aerialist peered over the edge of the roof. He dodged through an archway to the lane beyond, and ran to his right. Instead of running straight along it, he scaled another wall into another yard, through a gate and into a yard, then a wider lane.

He knew these streets like he knew the patterns of lines on Charlie's palm. The aerialist did not. There were no sounds of pursuit; no hue and cry had been raised. He was very much alone on the frosty, sooty London evening. He slowed to a brisk walk and headed back toward Highgate. He'd not brought a horse or carriage with him, and the walk was a long one.

So he ran. Instead of allowing his mind to wander at will, he forced himself to stay alert, to listen and focus on the task at hand. He'd almost missed the piece of paper in the boot, now tucked into his pocket. That was sloppy. He'd also almost been caught. That was unfortunate. On the other hand, it was also exhilarating. He'd not had a good chase across rooftops in an age.

Lichfield Towers was in darkness when he arrived.

Nobody waited up for him. He hadn't asked them to, and yet he almost wished he had.

He shook off those thoughts and poured himself a brandy in the library. By the light of the candles, he dug the note out of his pocket and read it. It was an address. One he knew well.

Harcourt House, Mayfair. Julia's home, and Andrew Buchanan's.

CHAPTER 4

*L*incoln was a coward. It wasn't a word he liked to associate with himself, but on this occasion, he could admit it. He hunched into his coat on the street opposite Harcourt House, his hood pulled low, and waited for Julia to leave. More than an hour later, his patience was rewarded as the front door opened and Millard the butler handed her an umbrella. She descended the steps and strolled up the street. Once she was gone from sight, Lincoln approached the house.

Millard answered his knock. "Lady Harcourt is not at home, sir."

"I wish to see Mr. Buchanan," Lincoln said.

"He's not available to callers."

Meaning he was probably still in bed. Lincoln checked his pocket watch. It was almost midday. "Inform Mr. Buchanan that he will make himself available to discuss Ela. If he's not down within fifteen minutes, I'll come up to his room and drag him out of bed by the ankles."

Millard didn't blink an eye. He merely stepped aside to allow Lincoln in. "May I take your coat, sir?"

Fifteen minutes later, Buchanan ambled into the drawing room. He looked as if someone *had* dragged him out of bed by the ankles. His fair hair was flat on one side and stuck out from his head on the other. He rubbed bloodshot eyes and stifled a yawn.

"Bloody early, ain't it, Fitzroy?"

"No."

Buchanan crossed to the window and looked out. He winced and rubbed his eyes again, even though the day wasn't bright. "You're right. Not too early for a drink at all." He poured a snifter of brandy and offered it to Lincoln.

Lincoln shook his head and Buchanan sipped from the glass. "I believe you know Ela, one of Barnum and Bailey's dancers," Lincoln said.

Buchanan smirked. "I *know* her. Speaking of girls, where's your fiancée? She's not with you today?"

Julia hadn't told him? "Charlie no longer lives with me."

Buchanan lowered the glass and blinked slowly, as if waking from a dream. "You don't say. Interesting."

"Why?"

Buchanan swirled the liquid around the snifter. "Does this mean you're no longer engaged?"

Blood surged along Lincoln's veins. He forced himself to remain still, and to think. A suitable answer came to him after several thumping heartbeats. "Charlie is too young to get married."

"Hardly. Girls younger than her have been hitched, or promised." Buchanan's smirk reappeared, more twisted than before. "Besides, she's hardly innocent, given her background. Probably has more experience than me. I wouldn't mind finding out what the little vixen—"

Lincoln grabbed the turd's throat, cutting off the flow of verbal vomit spewing from his mouth. Buchanan choked out something inaudible, and his face turned a satisfying shade of red.

"If you disparage her again," Lincoln snarled in Buchanan's ear, "I will castrate you and serve your balls to you on a platter. Do you understand?"

The purple veins on Buchanan's temple stood out in bas-relief. He attempted a nod.

Lincoln let him go and watched as Buchanan fell to his knees, one hand at his throat, the other holding the snifter steady so that none of the liquid spilled.

A movement by the door caught Lincoln's attention. Millard stood there, his steady gaze on his master. How much had he seen? After a moment, he merely said, "Is there anything you require, sir?"

"No," Lincoln said, not caring if Millard had addressed him or Buchanan. "Get up," he ordered Buchanan when Millard backed out of the drawing room and shut the doors, despite not being asked to. "I have questions about Ela."

"If you want me to talk, you shouldn't've tried to bloody kill me," Buchanan rasped.

"If I wanted to kill you, you would be dead." Lincoln waited while Buchanan got to his feet, drank the rest of his drink, and poured himself another.

By the time he sat in the armchair, his color had returned to its usual washed-out pallor, although his throat remained red. "What about Ela?"

"You know her intimately."

Buchanan held his glass up in salute. "And?"

"And did you know that she was also intimate with another circus performer by the name of Patrick O'Neill?"

"A mick?" He snorted then winced and rubbed his throat. After a long sip, he said, "Thought she had better taste than that. He's not one of those freaks, is he?"

"He was the strong man."

Buchanan paused, the glass near his lips. "Was?"

"He died two nights ago."

Buchanan nodded thoughtfully then took another sip. "Then she'll be more available now. Twice a week isn't enough."

Lincoln waited while Buchanan finished the rest of his drink. What had Julia ever seen in this parasite? Perhaps he'd been less of a prick when she'd first met him at The Alhambra. Perhaps their prior connection, and her subsequent rejection of him in favor of his father, made her feel guilty enough to allow him to stay on at Harcourt House. Then again, Lincoln wasn't sure if guilt was an emotion she was capable of feeling.

"What does the fellow's death have to do with me?" Buchanan drawled.

"Did you kill him?"

"No! Do you think I'm jealous of a greasy mick freak? I didn't even know about him until now."

Lincoln believed him. The man was easy to read, and Lincoln's senses told him he had nothing to hide. Buchanan hadn't killed O'Neill. "He knew about you," Lincoln said. "I found this address among his things."

"Blimey. Do you think *he* was jealous of *me*?"

"It's possible. It's also possible that he was killed before he had a chance to come here and confront you, if that were his intention."

Buchanan swallowed and touched the red mark across his throat. "Thank God for that."

"Have you seen anyone lurking outside lately? Have you been followed?"

"Not that I am aware. What did he look like?"

"Regular height and average build with brown hair. He sported a beard and moustache, and would have had an Irish accent."

"Doesn't sound familiar." He frowned. "Wouldn't the circus strong man be, well, strongly built? I thought a thick build would be the order of the day."

"O'Neill's strength was quite ordinary. His feats were a result of his supernatural power. He could move objects with his mind."

Buchanan leaned forward and held the empty glass by the tips of his fingers. His eyes flared. "Incredible. What a power to have! Image the things one could do."

Imagine the things that could be done if someone like Buchanan had powers. It was why it was so important to document the lineage of supernaturals and know where each one was at all times. Lincoln might not always like the committee members, but he agreed with their philosophy and that of the ministry on the whole. Having supernaturals living among regular folk had the potential for danger, if certain powers were controlled by the wrong people. It was why he'd told Charlie not to let anyone see her use her necromancy, and why he'd not told a soul where she'd gone.

Lincoln took the liberty of pouring himself a snifter of brandy. He drank it and set the glass back on the sideboard. It didn't make him feel any better.

"I say, are you listening?" Buchanan said.

Lincoln turned and gripped the edge of the sideboard at his back. He hadn't heard a word. "Go on."

"I was telling you about the strange thing that happened to me last week. On Tuesday, I think it was. I'd spent the previous night in the arms of the delightfully supple Ela at our usual meeting place."

"Which is?"

"A dreary little establishment in Kensington where rooms can be rented by the hour." He screwed up his nose and snorted. "The landlord resembles a rat. Can't recall his name now. Anyway, I left after we…you know…and came home a little after dawn. I was almost at the steps here when I slipped over on the pavement." He looked at Lincoln, waiting for a response.

"You were drunk."

"Not very. Besides, I can drink a bottle of champagne and still walk a straight line, I'll have you know." He sniffed then frowned at his empty glass. "It was strange. The ground was dry, I didn't trip, and I had an odd sensation of my legs buckling under me. Then there was the laughter."

"Go on."

"I thought I heard a man laugh. When I looked up to give him a piece of my mind, there was only one fellow nearby and he was walking away."

"Describe him."

"He wore a hood and I couldn't see his face, but he was neither tall nor short, fat nor thin." He shrugged. "If there was something distinguishing about him, I would have taken more note, but I forgot about him instantly."

"Which direction did he head?"

"West."

If it had been O'Neill, and his revenge upon his rival had merely been to make him fall down, then Lincoln doubted jealousy was a motive for his murder. O'Neill hadn't confronted Buchanan over his affection for Ela, so it was unlikely he would confront any of her other lovers, if she had any. It was looking less and less like O'Neill's death had a logical explanation at all.

And more and more like he was killed for being a supernatural.

* * *

LINCOLN KNEW before he reached Lichfield that something was amiss. He couldn't pinpoint what it was, but it felt like a change in the air, a disturbance. If he had to guess, he would say that someone new had arrived at the house. But Lichfield Towers never had callers except committee members.

He entered via the back door and went to the kitchen directly. Doyle jumped to his feet and stumbled through a greeting. He quickly put his hands behind his back, perhaps to hide his forearms. He'd removed his jacket and rolled up his shirtsleeves to do the polishing.

Cook said nothing, just glared from his position by the stove. It was his usual response of late. Gus barely lifted his gaze from the carrots he peeled at the table. He seemed to be warring with a smile. Lincoln had a bad feeling about the visitor.

"Who's here?" he asked Doyle.

Doyle blew out a breath as if he were fortifying himself. "Lady Vickers, sir."

Seth's mother. Lincoln had forgotten she was due to arrive from America. He had agreed that she could stay at Lichfield until she found a position as companion to one of her friends, but that had been before Charlie left. Now he would have preferred to be alone with only the servants for company.

"Where's Seth?" he asked.

"Helping her ladyship settle into her room," Doyle said.

"Which one?"

"The yellow room furthest from your suite, sir."

"Gus, I want you and Seth to join me in my study after he's finished with Lady Vickers."

"Sir," Doyle said as Lincoln went to leave. "An invitation from Lady Harcourt arrived a few minutes ago. Shall I bring it up to you?"

"Bring it up with luncheon." He strode out of the kitchen. "And wine."

He took the servants' stairs to the second level. Seth's

raised voice echoed along the corridor from the other end of the house, where Lady Vickers now resided. A booming female voice responded. Lincoln retreated to his own rooms and shut the door.

He settled at his desk and contemplated his next course of action. O'Neill's death looked like it was due to his supernatural powers. But with no clues as to the killer's identity, or that of the man who'd hired him, Lincoln had to return to the information from Billy the Bolter. He didn't like to rely on others, but he had no choice. He had to trust that Billy hadn't simply made up a story to get paid. Lincoln hoped his reputation was fearsome enough to deter false claims.

Doyle brought up luncheon and the invitation to Julia's ball. It was to be held that night. Clearly Lincoln's new status as a single man had secured this last minute inclusion.

"Will there be a reply, sir?" Doyle asked.

"Not yet."

"Very well."

He opened the door and a woman's voice ran clear through the house like a bell. Doyle cast Lincoln a sympathetic grimace then stepped aside to allow a woman dressed head to toe in deep black to enter. Seth came in behind her, a harried look in his eyes.

Lincoln stood and bowed. "Lady Vickers, I assume."

She gave him a simple nod. "Mr. Fitzroy, I want to thank you for inviting me to stay."

"Inviting?" He shot a glare at Seth.

Seth looked like he wanted to turn and leave. If he did, Lincoln would chase him and haul him back by his collar. He wasn't doing this alone.

"Of course it won't be for long," Lady Vickers went on with a wave of her gloved hand. "Once word gets out that I have returned to London, I expect the invitations from my friends to flow in. It would be cruel of me to refuse, particularly when their country houses are so much larger than Lichfield Towers. Why, I feel as if I am under your feet here."

Lincoln stared. He wasn't sure what to say. *Congratulations? I hope you're not too disappointed in the size of the house?* It had been large enough until she arrived.

Lady Vickers seemed to be waiting for him to speak, but he kept quiet in case he said the wrong thing. This was a woman who appeared to be comfortable with polite small talk, and Lincoln had found that area of his education as lacking as his understanding of people. She was everything he'd come to expect in an English lady of a certain age. She was quite tall, like Seth, with a formidable figure. She wouldn't be easy to knock off her feet. She wore mourning, but whether that was for her husband or her lover, he couldn't be sure. Perhaps both. The hem was a little frayed and the clothes themselves simple in style with no embellishments. She touched the ring finger on her left hand. It was bare, like all of her fingers, and Lincoln suspected the action was born from habit. She wore no jewelry, not even earbobs.

Lincoln didn't need those pieces of evidence to know she'd fallen on hard times. Seth had explained the family's destitution when they'd met, and Lincoln had researched them thoroughly before employing him. Indeed, little research had been required. He'd already witnessed the circumstances Seth had been reduced to.

Lincoln had saved Seth from auctioning himself off amid a crowd full of men at a gentleman's club. Prior to Lincoln stepping in, the highest bidder had been an aging gentleman whose younger wife was known for her sexual appetites. The husband was equally known for his—with other men. Lincoln didn't care what the couple had in store for their prize. For all he knew, Seth had wanted them to win. It wasn't sympathy that had led Lincoln to bid for Seth.

It had been Seth's skill in the boxing ring that had first

brought him to Lincoln's notice. He could fight either Queensberry Rules or bareknuckle and knock his opponent to the ground in mere seconds. Many pugilists merely stood in one spot and tried to pummel the opposition, taking just as many blows as they gave. But Seth avoided contact by dodging and ducking, something that allowed him to get into a position to take his opponent by surprise. His sequence of moves were never the same, and this variety meant he could outwit even the strongest fighters on the circuit.

The fighting had definitely brought Seth to Lincoln's notice, but it was his other qualities altogether that secured his decision to employ him. He admired that Seth had been prepared to do anything to pay off his father's debts, including lower himself to a point that no man, let alone a nobleman, should lower himself to. That showed honor and a strength of character rarely seen in a man of his class. After Lincoln made the decision to employ him, it was merely a matter of waiting for the opportune moment—a moment when Seth would be grateful that Lincoln had stepped in and saved him when he did. That moment had come at the auction. Seth had indeed been grateful, and he became the perfect employee.

Until Charlie came along. With her wit, courage, and friendly manner, she'd quickly won over Seth, Gus and Cook. Ever since Lincoln had sent her away, Seth could barely even speak to Lincoln, and he was certainly no longer grateful.

"My son says there is a larger suite of rooms on this level," Lady Vickers was saying.

Lincoln's gaze slid to Seth's. Seth swallowed heavily.

"May I have them?" she went on.

"No," Lincoln said.

"But he tells me that your fiancée no longer lives here, and so I assumed—"

"You assumed incorrectly. The suite is unavailable."

Behind her, a strange smile crept across Seth's face. "The yellow room will have to do, Mother. I'm sure it's comparable in size to the one your footman secured for you in New York."

She stiffened at her son's barb. It would seem that Seth wanted to punish his mother for running off to America with the family's second footman, leaving Seth with debts to settle. Lincoln couldn't blame him for that.

"Seth tells me there are no maids here," Lady Vickers said.

"That is correct," Lincoln said.

Her smooth forehead dipped into a frown. "But who will see to my personal needs?"

"Who saw to them in America?"

"Oh, the Americans are different." She waved her hand. "They don't like to keep maids."

Lincoln had been to America. New York's upper classes kept as many servants as the English gentry. It was more likely that Lady Vickers and her footman lover couldn't afford one on his wages. Lincoln wondered if the footman was indeed dead, or if she had left him to return to a country where she assumed people still recognized her and respected the Vickers title. If so, she was in for a shock. Seth may have paid off all his father's debts, but the name was as firmly stuck in the mire, as it had been when she left. She needed to take the blame for that as much as her late husband, in Lincoln's opinion.

"I have no objection to you appointing your own maid," he told her. "As long as she stays out of my way and that of my men. Seth will see to the expense." He gave Seth what he hoped was a knowing nod.

Seth must have understood that Lincoln would give him an allowance to cover the wages of a maid, because his lips parted and nothing came out. For once, the man took several moments to respond. "Er, yes, sir. I'll see to it. Thank you, sir...for reminding me that I will see to it, that is." He cleared his throat and smiled at his mother, only to have it wither when she frowned at him.

She turned back to Lincoln. "You call my son by his first name?"

While Lady Vickers knew that Seth lived in Lincoln's house, she probably didn't know that he was effectively a servant. How would Charlie respond to such a question?

"That's what friends do," he said lamely. No, Charlie wouldn't have said that.

"A friend of a peer calls the peer by his title, in this case, Vickers. The peer would then respond with the fellow's first or last name, not 'sir.'" If her lip curled up any more it would disappear into her nostril.

Since he could think of nothing to say, Lincoln simply nodded at Seth, in the hope he would understand that Lincoln wanted the woman gone from his rooms. "Seth, if you're finished, I wish to speak with you."

"Yes, sir."

Lincoln suspected he'd added the "sir" to rile his mother. The man's lack of pomposity was another reason Lincoln liked him.

Lady Vickers bristled. Her back went rigid in the same way that Julia's did when she felt slighted. "What time is the dinner gong?"

"We only use the gong when we have guests," Lincoln said. "Dinner can be at whatever hour you like. Simply inform Cook. Or inform Doyle, who will inform Cook."

"But what time do you prefer, Mr. Fitzroy? I don't want to upset your routine."

"You won't. I eat in here at odd hours. You are free to do the same in your own rooms."

"Oh." She touched her ring finger again. "I had hoped to eat in the dining room."

"Then eat there. I don't mind."

"Alone?"

"Ask Seth to join you." He didn't emphasize the name, yet Lady Vickers's spine straightened even more. Behind her, Seth smirked again. Lincoln almost nodded at him, as if they'd shared a private joke. "I have work to do, and I need your son, madam. Seth, fetch Gus."

Seth left. After a moment, his mother left too, muttering under her breath about England having gone to the dogs since her departure. Lincoln ate lunch while he waited and tried to think of his next course of action. It wasn't easy reining in his thoughts, and he finally gave up. Hopefully discussing everything with his men would help him focus.

"She wants to restore the family name," he heard Seth tell Gus as the men approached the open door.

Gus snorted. "How, when she ain't got no ready to buy friends?"

"Try telling her that! She seems to think they'll accept her with open arms because she's a Vickers. That's not the worst of it. Once she has re-established herself, she plans on finding me a wife."

Gus was still laughing when he entered ahead of Seth. It quickly died, and he stood like a statue by the door. The joke wasn't to be shared with Lincoln.

It was a little early for liquor, but Lincoln poured two glasses of brandy and offered them to the men. Gus accepted but Seth crossed his arms. After a sigh, Gus handed the glass back. Resisting the urge to drain the contents himself, Lincoln set the glasses down on his desk.

"O'Neill wasn't killed because of his relationship with Ela," he told them.

"How do you know?" Gus asked.

"I just do." When both men exchanged glances, he added, "O'Neill knew about Buchanan and Ela, but his revenge took the form of a harmless joke. He made Buchanan slip over on the street then walked away, laughing. I have no reason to believe he was going to confront Buchanan, and Buchanan wasn't lying when he told me he didn't know about Ela and O'Neill."

"Again, how do you know?" Seth demanded.

Lincoln made his decision quickly. He didn't know if he could trust these men anymore, but if he was going to keep them at Lichfield in his employ, he needed to be someone *they* could trust. And that meant revealing something about himself he'd only ever revealed to Charlie. "I have some capacity to know when others are telling the truth or not. It doesn't work on everyone, but it did work on Buchanan. He told me no lies."

Seth lowered his arms and took a step forward. Gus's hand whipped out, stopping his friend from getting too close. What did he think Lincoln would do?

"How do you have this ability?" Seth asked.

"My mother was a seer. I seem to have inherited it from her, but in a limited capacity."

Seth didn't look like this revelation made him trust Lincoln more. Quite the opposite, in fact. Lincoln was no expert, but his stiff stance was decidedly hostile. "Can you tell when *we're* lying?"

"No."

Seth studied Lincoln, and Lincoln bore it until Seth gave up with a grunt.

"Seers can predict the future," Gus said. "Can you?"

"No. My powers only extend to…feelings."

Both men burst out laughing.

Lincoln could see how it would be amusing from their perspective, although he didn't think it *that* funny. "What I mean is, I know when someone new is in the house, for example, or when someone is missing." He didn't tell them that these "feelings" were strongest in regard to Charlie. Mentioning her name could prove volatile.

They both took a moment to digest this, then Seth said, "If a jealous lover didn't kill O'Neill, could there be another motive?"

"I haven't found one."

"Excepting the fact that he was a supernatural, and perhaps killed because of his powers."

"Excepting that." Lincoln waited while the men considered this. "Billy the Bolter's information is my—our—only link to the man who is hiring killers to assassinate supernaturals."

"But he didn't tell us much," Gus said. "Nothing we can use, anyway."

"Only that the fellow is a toff," Seth said.

"We can be almost sure that the person has access to our archives, or has records of their own." Lincoln waited as both men staggered under the weight of this news. He held out the glasses of brandy to them.

They both drank the contents in one gulp. Gus slammed the empty glass down on the desk and swore. "The committee."

"Will you confront them?" Seth asked.

"Not yet," Lincoln said. "Not until I'm sure."

"How will you be sure?"

"Through observation and investigation, beginning with attending Julia's Christmas ball tonight."

"You hate balls," Gus said.

"I didn't say I wanted to enjoy myself." Lincoln nodded at Seth. "You're coming. Bring your mother."

Seth's face fell. "Do I have to?" he whined.

"Yes."

"You want her to interrogate the committee members too?" Gus asked.

"I thought she could use the event as a way of announcing her return to London. She can reacquaint herself with her old friends."

Seth's face fell even more. "Has she been invited?"

"Tell her she has been. Julia won't mind. She and scandal like to flirt with one another, after all."

That almost earned a smile from Seth. Gus chuckled. "Wish I could go to watch."

"You will drive us, then keep warm in the mews. The servants know you and might offer some gossip. If you speak to the inside servants, ask them who has accessed the attic archives in recent times."

"Right, sir."

They both looked enthused by the prospect of being involved in the investigation. Good. Perhaps this was a turning point. Perhaps they'd given up on Charlie ever coming home.

"You're both dismissed." Lincoln turned away.

Even though he couldn't see them, he knew they were gesturing to one another and urging the other to speak. In the end, it was Seth who cleared his throat. Lincoln braced himself. He didn't need to have a seer's powers to know what the conversation would be about.

"Her birthday is only days away," Seth said.

Charlie's nineteenth birthday had been on his mind too lately, among other things. "And?"

"And we wish to send her a gift. We can't do so without knowing where she is."

"I won't be giving you her location."

"You have to!" Gus snapped. "She's our friend."

"She's like a sister," Seth added in a rough voice. He sounded like he was barely holding in his temper.

Lincoln leaned his knuckles on the desk and bowed his head. "I cannot risk anyone finding her."

Silence. He resisted the urge to glance over his shoulder to see if they were looking at him or gesturing to each other again.

"So you *do* still care for her wellbeing," Seth finally said in quiet tones.

"I knew it." Gus sounded pleased.

Lincoln straightened and turned to face them. "Sending her a gift would only give her false hope that she will return."

Gus gave him a blank look. He shrugged. "But she will return. After you've caught the killer, you'll fetch her and bring her home."

Lincoln gripped the desk behind him and shook his head. "She's a distraction to me. I cannot afford distractions."

Seth's fist shot out, but Lincoln deflected it. He grabbed Seth's arm, twisted it, and forced him to the ground. The maneuver would have caused pain, but to Seth's credit, he merely winced. He didn't try to resist.

Gus, however, decided to fight on his friend's behalf. He wrapped one muscular arm around Lincoln's throat and squeezed. With his knee still in Seth's back, Lincoln let go and grasped onto Gus's hair. Lincoln could break his neck, but he chose to pull out a fistful of hair instead.

Gus let go and clutched his scalp. He reeled backward, out of reach. "I'm bleeding!"

Lincoln stood and held out his hand to Seth. Seth ignored it and got to his feet on his own. He stepped up to Lincoln, his fists at his sides, a murderous scowl on his face.

"You are the most selfish, cold-hearted prick I've ever met," he snarled through his teeth. "When the killer is caught, I'm leaving Lichfield. I no longer want to work for someone who can banish the only person who cares about him without batting an eye."

Lincoln was too far away from the desk to use it as support, so he had to stand there and concentrate very hard on being still, on not blinking or showing these men that he felt sick to his core every time he thought about Charlie being far away.

Fortunately he didn't need to order them to get out. They left of their own accord, although Gus couldn't resist a parting shot. "I hope your shriveled heart keeps you warm at night."

"Close the door," Lincoln told him.

Gus's top lip curled up, but he did as ordered.

Alone again, Lincoln sank onto the chair at his desk and dragged both hands through his hair and down his face. With shaking fingers, he removed the key to Charlie's room from his pocket and placed it in his top drawer. Then he locked it.

CHAPTER 5

"*Y*our hair looks fine," Seth said yet again, as his mother patted her hair for the hundredth time. He had to shout to be heard above the rain attempting to smash through the carriage roof. The weather had turned vicious.

"Fine?" Lady Vickers continued to pat. "It needs to be better than fine."

"It is. It's lovely. Elegant." At his mother's continuing frown, Seth added, "Magnificent! Divine! Your new lady's maid is a marvel."

"She'll do. There appears to be a shortage of quality servants in the city."

"Bella was the only one I could find available to begin immediately." Seth tried to move his legs but found his mother's voluminous ink-black skirts in the way. He gave up and tucked his feet closer to his seat.

"How *did* you find her, I wonder?"

Lincoln watched mother and son exchange hard glares and wished he was somewhere else. Anywhere else. He knew how Seth had found Bella—she was one of his many mistresses—and it seemed his mother had guessed.

"Luck," was all Seth said.

Lady Vickers tucked her hand back into her fur muff. It seemed she wasn't so destitute that she'd sold off the evening gown, only the jewels. Her ears, throat and fingers were quite bare. "I do hope she won't be a distraction to the other servants. She is, after all, very young and pretty." Was she speaking to Seth or Lincoln? Lincoln decided not to answer.

"Not that young." Seth's mutter was barely audible above the rain. "She's twenty, at least."

His mother's lips pinched. Her gaze turned sharp. "You're not to look at her, Seth. I know what you're like, and she's not for you."

"So it's perfectly acceptable for you to fraternize with the staff but not me."

The baroness thrust out her noble chin as far as it would go. "I did my duty. I married well the first time and didn't *fraternize* with anyone until after my husband died."

"'The first time?'" Seth paled. "Mother...tell me you didn't *marry* the footman."

Lady Vickers turned to the window, her chin somewhat lower. Seth had his answer. He sat back in the leather seat, deflated.

Lincoln might hate balls, but Harcourt House couldn't come fast enough. The air in the carriage was frostier than outside. One of Julia's footmen opened the door, handed Seth an umbrella, and stepped aside as Seth climbed out. He assisted his mother and they walked up the steps arm in arm, as if they hadn't just argued. Lincoln didn't want to miss Julia's reaction upon seeing them, but he needed to have a quick word with Gus first. He accepted the second umbrella from the footman and handed his flask up to Gus.

Gus took a moment before he shook his head. "Got me

own, sir." He patted the chest of his coat. Despite the weatherproof coat with its multiple capes and the wide-brimmed hat, Gus was thoroughly wet.

"You might need another," Lincoln told him, holding the flask higher.

Gus took it with a nod. "Thank you, sir."

Another coach pulled up behind, and Gus drove off. Millard took Lincoln's umbrella, coat and hat in the hall, then Lincoln headed upstairs. He joined Seth and Lady Vickers in the ballroom, where they had stopped to speak with Julia at the entrance. Lady Vickers was regaling their hostess with the tale of her sea voyage. Julia appeared to be listening with polite interest.

"Thank you for the invitation, Julia," Lady Vickers said. "It's most unexpected but very considerate indeed." Like her son, Lady Vickers could turn on the charm when she wanted to. Her superior manner seemed to come naturally, as if she believed she had a right to be there. It would take a socially confident woman to turn her away. "My return to London must be quite the sensation if *you* heard about it," Lady Vickers finished.

Julia's smile broadened. She never smiled that much. Not sincerely anyway. "I'm delighted that you accepted my invitation. And you too, Seth."

Seth bowed over her hand, but he didn't hide his distaste. Ever since witnessing Julia's cruel behavior toward Charlie, Seth had gone cold toward his occasional lover. The only indication that she noticed was a slight tightening of her lips as he straightened.

"I do hope you'll spare a dance or two for my son," Lady Vickers went on with a gleam in her eye. "He tells me that he finds you to be a rare gem in this city, and that he hopes to get to know you better."

Julia flushed ever so slightly but her smile remained.

Seth's smile held a darkly wicked edge. "You are correct, Mother. Julia is rare, indeed. I can honestly say that I've never met anyone like her before."

Lady Vickers beamed. "Isn't he charming?"

"But I assure you, Mother, Julia and I are already acquainted as deeply as we both would like to be." He bowed again to Julia, so deeply as to be mocking. "It's kind of you to take pity on we poor unfortunate outcasts. We'll try not to embarrass you, but I can't make any promises. You know what I'm like."

Lady Vickers was left staring open-mouthed at Seth as he strode off. She followed him without a word, and they disappeared into the crowd. Julia stood stony-faced and immobile.

Lincoln stepped into their place. "Good evening, Julia." There were several bland pleasantries he could have uttered about her dress, the house, or the weather, but he didn't feel like making the effort.

"I'll be a laughing stock for inviting her," she whispered. She turned hard, glittering eyes onto Lincoln. "I suppose she's my punishment."

"No, she's not." He turned and walked off, hoping she assumed a worse punishment was yet to come.

He nodded at a group of gentlemen as he moved farther into the room. Julia had decorated the ballroom with hothouse flowers blooming out of season, and clusters of silver and blue ribbons adorned the walls, connected by swathes of more ribbons. The facets of the lead crystal candelabras and chandeliers provided a dazzling example of light dispersion and refraction. Julia didn't do anything in half measures.

He spotted Seth surrounded by people of both sexes, most of them young and already on their way to being drunk. A mature woman standing a little to one side tried to catch his attention with a rapid flutter of her fan. Seth extracted himself from the girls clinging to each of his arms and went to speak to the woman, much to her delight. If the diamonds dripping from her person were any indication, she was wealthy indeed. Lady Vickers was nowhere to be seen.

Lincoln scanned the faces and saw Andrew Buchanan talking with three gentlemen, their gazes all on the doorway leading to an adjoining room. Buchanan shrugged then nodded. One of the fellows slapped him on the back, shoving him toward the door. Buchanan moved off, and the three men grinned then followed.

Lincoln went to listen in. He'd spent much of the afternoon listening to conversations in pubs and speaking with his contacts again, but he'd come home with no new information. By the end of the day, he was quite sure the killer hadn't made further contact with anyone else. It would seem he was satisfied with the gunman he'd hired to kill O'Neill.

It only remained to be seen who was next on his list, unless Lincoln could stop him first.

The room adjoining the ballroom was quieter and smoky. Card players in deep concentration clustered around the tables. Buchanan sauntered up to one lady, her back to the door. Her fair hair had slipped a little from its arrangement and she wore no jewels at her ears or neck. So Lady Vickers was a card player. Lincoln wondered what she wagered with. Perhaps Seth had given her some money. Lincoln watched as Buchanan touched the back of her bare neck and skimmed his thumb along her shoulder. He bent down to whisper something in his ear.

"Why, sir, you're disturbing my concentration." Lady Vickers fluttered her hand of cards at her face, and leaned away from him. It was such a slight shifting of her weight that most would not have noticed it, but Lincoln saw, as did Buchanan.

He looked as if he were about to walk off when one of his

friends cleared his throat. Buchanan appeared to make up his mind about something. "My apologies," he drawled, hand on his heart. Behind him, his three friends snickered. "It's Lady Vickers, is it not?"

She held out her hand and he kissed it. "Are we acquainted, sir?"

"We are now. Shall I assist you to win this round? I'm an excellent player."

"Are you? Then, by all means, join in." She indicated a vacant seat to her right. "I do love a challenge."

She threw in her hand and pushed her wagered coins to the player opposite. A new round was dealt, which she won. She also won the next two, and Buchanan declared that he was out. He got up from the table amid protests from Lady Vickers, who claimed to have enjoyed playing against him.

"Of course you did," Buchanan muttered. "You fleeced me."

She laughed, as did her companions.

Buchanan rejoined his friends, who were also laughing. As they walked off, he handed them each a bank note. Lady Vickers watched them go with a satisfied curve to her lips. She caught sight of Lincoln, nodded, and turned back to her game.

Lincoln returned to the ballroom where the band struck up a waltz. He spotted each of the committee members, conversing in separate groups. If he wanted to investigate them, he needed to join them. It was going to be a long night.

Julia approached and he allowed her to intercept him. "Why did you come, Lincoln?" she said, toying with the diamond and sapphire necklace at her throat.

"I've been told I need to socialize more." He watched Lord Marchbank over the top of her head. The nobleman appeared to be listening intently to the fellow on his right, a

Liberal politician. "Apparently all the important decisions are made at parties."

"Dinner parties, mostly. Why this sudden interest in politics? You never used to care about the government, and I admit that I rather saw you as above all that."

"I wasn't referring to politics. If you'll excuse me, I need to mingle."

"You are mingling. With me." She sipped her champagne and watched him over the rim of the glass with a practiced flutter of her eyelashes.

"You and I are through *mingling*, Julia."

She lowered the glass. "So you keep saying."

He couldn't tell if she believed they were over or not. She seemed to think he would change his mind again. Sending Charlie away and breaking off their engagement had probably reignited Julia's hopes.

"Miss Overton hasn't been able to take her eyes off you." She nodded at the Overton girl, standing in her mother's shadow with a gaggle of ladies. "Why don't you ask her to dance?"

"I don't dance."

"If you want to mingle, you must learn to dance."

"I didn't say I *can't* dance."

"Then you have no excuses."

"Except that I don't want to dance. The girl needs no encouragement." It would be cruel to dance with her if he had no intentions toward her. But it was in Julia's nature to be cruel to others if it benefitted her. Marrying him off to the guileless and obedient Miss Overton would clear the path for a woman who wanted to be his mistress but not his wife.

"I don't know why you resist her." She smiled at Miss Overton who glanced behind her, thinking someone else had caught Julia's interest. "She would make the perfect wife. Her family is well connected and wealthy; she's healthy, pretty and young, just the way you like them."

"Don't," he growled.

"And she's a far more agreeable girl than...others. You could manage her very well, and I dare say, after a year, you would have molded her into whatever shape you desire. As long as you use a delicate touch and don't frighten her, that is." The eyes she turned on him were as cold and hard as the gems at her throat.

He turned his back on her and wove his way through the crowd. He joined Lord Marchbank and the politician but quickly realized their discussion wouldn't tell him anything important.

After ten minutes, Marchbank accepted a drink from his wife with a "Thank you, m'dear." She nodded at Lincoln and smiled tentatively.

Lincoln extended his hand before he changed his mind. "Dance with me, madam." He winced. It sounded like he was commanding her, not asking.

The conversation around them stopped. Lincoln watched Lord Marchbank in his peripheral vision, but he didn't seem to mind another man asking his wife to dance.

Lady Marchbank took Lincoln's hand. "I would be delighted, Mr. Fitzroy. Thank you."

They waited on the edge of the dance floor for the set to end and another to strike up. Lady Marchbank was the eldest dancer to take the floor. Some onlookers stared and whispered, but she either didn't notice or ignored them. She was a little younger than her husband and still a beauty, with high cheekbones, delicate features, and silver hair. She was an excellent dancer and all but floated in Lincoln's arms. Her small smile lifted Lincoln's mood a little, until he remembered he had to think of something to talk about.

"The weather is terrible tonight," he began.

"Atrocious," she agreed. "I comfort myself that it must be even worse at March Hall. It's always colder in Yorkshire than London."

Charlie was in Yorkshire. Lincoln hadn't seen the School for Wayward Girls in person, but he knew the building had once been home to a noble family who'd sold it to the headmistress. There would be fireplaces—dozens of them—so the rooms must be warm. Even if there were only one, the school would be infinitely better than the abandoned buildings Charlie had lived in the last few winters.

His stomach knotted as it always did when he thought about her struggling to survive on the streets. This time of year must have been hell. He'd spent days in the cold of winter, sometimes in the city and other times in the countryside, both as a child and an adult, but never more than that, and he'd known a warm fire, bed and food waited for him at the end of the ordeal.

He tore his thoughts back to the present. "Do you spend much time at March Hall?" he asked as they twirled past another couple.

"Very little. Ewan prefers London. Business, you know." Her smile implied something, but Lincoln didn't know what.

Lincoln wasn't sure how to proceed next. Short of asking her directly if she knew her husband was behind the murders of the supernaturals, he was at a loss. "Nasty business, the death of the circus strongman," he tried.

"It is. Ewan is very distressed by it, and the other recent murders."

He almost propelled her into a passing couple in his surprise, but just managed to steer her clear of a collision. She must know about the connection between the deaths. "You've spoken about it with your husband?"

"Of course. I am aware of the ministry, Mr. Fitzroy, and the work you do there." Her smile reached her blue eyes then turned grim. "I hope you find the person responsible before another life is taken."

"I'm trying my best."

"I don't doubt it." Her silence felt weighty as they twirled again. "When you do catch the murderer, will you bring Miss Holloway back here to London?"

"I sent her away permanently."

"That is not what I asked."

The music ended, saving him from replying. He bowed to her. She curtsied in response and allowed him to lead her off the dance floor.

"Ewan is worried about you, you know," she said before he deposited her with her husband.

"He shouldn't be," Lincoln said. "I have no distractions now. My sole focus is my work."

"Is that so? Then why haven't you caught the killer yet?"

He blinked and concentrated on keeping his breathing even, despite the tightening of his chest. "It's not that easy."

"Very well, I'll grant you that. Let me put it another way. Why did you ask me to dance then not question me about the people here tonight?"

He stared at her. Was she a seer? Or simply clever?

"That is why you asked me to dance, isn't it?" she pressed.

"I…perhaps I simply wished to dance with you."

"I would believe that of some gentlemen, but not of you, Mr. Fitzroy. It took me a few moments to think it through, but when I realized your true motive, it began to make sense. You think someone here tonight is guilty of the murders?"

"I'm not sure."

"I understand the need for secrecy, but if you want to know anything about anyone in this room, you only have to ask. Julia would be more than happy to help too, of course. She will probably know more than me. I don't attend as many social events as she does."

Lincoln presented Lady Marchbank to her husband, bowed again, and thanked her for the dance. As he walked away, he couldn't help but be relieved that he hadn't asked her directly about Marchbank. She would have become suspicious, and Lincoln couldn't risk her alerting her husband, or anyone on the committee, to his concerns.

He spent the remainder of the evening avoiding Julia and Mrs. Overton, who must have decided, once again, that he was worth pursuing for her daughter. He couldn't think why. He was hardly good husband material for any woman, let alone Miss Overton. The evening was quickly turning into a waste of time, and he was contemplating leaving early when Seth approached. Two females and one whey-faced gentleman stepped doubly fast behind him to match his long strides.

"Gilly and his wife are acting suspiciously," Seth whispered in Lincoln's ear.

"How so?"

"They're heading for a private assignation in the music room."

Lincoln looked at him.

Seth rolled his eyes. "No gentleman has a private assignation with his *own* wife. They must be up to something. I think you ought to sneak up on them and listen."

He left before Lincoln could question him further, his three friends following him like a tail.

The music room adjoined the ballroom, but Lincoln didn't find Lord and Lady Gillingham there. What he did find was a curtain billowing from a cold breeze. The doors leading to the balcony beyond were open. The rain must have stopped, but it would be icy outside, particularly for a lady dressed in eveningwear without her coat. Lincoln stood at the side of the curtain and listened to the couple arguing in low tones.

"This is absurd," Gillingham snapped. "You're making fools of us both."

"Nobody saw us." Lincoln recognized the voice as belonging to Lady Gillingham. He'd seen her earlier in a pale pink gown, her blonde hair arranged in the latest fashion. She was quite pretty, and several years younger than her husband. Lincoln wondered if theirs had been an arranged marriage.

"But it's freezing!" Gillingham whined.

"Then be quick."

"No. I absolutely refuse to do it here. It's degrading."

"I thought that's what you liked." Lady Gillingham's voice grated like nails down slate. "I thought the problem between us was that I wasn't debauched enough."

Lincoln silently cursed Seth. Had he known the Gillinghams really were leaving the ballroom for an assignation? It wouldn't surprise Lincoln to learn that Seth had sent him to watch them as a joke.

"You know what the problem between us is," Gillingham hissed, "and it has nothing to do with *me* and everything to do with your…true form."

True form?

"I know you find me ugly underneath this skin."

"I find you abhorrent. Disgusting. Ever since I discovered what you are back in the summer, I can't bring myself to look at you. You duped me, Harriet. You and your father. I don't like being tricked and I certainly don't like you."

Lincoln had to strain to hear her response. "You used to."

"That was before, when I thought you were…human."

"I am!"

Gillingham snorted. "Look at you. You're not even shivering."

"We are married in the eyes of the law, Gilly, and you have no grounds to divorce me, not without raising awkward questions I know you don't want asked. We might as well make the best of it for now."

"What do you want from me, Harriet? Why are you pestering me?"

"I want children. I want to bear your heir."

Gillingham made a choking sound. "Is this a joke?"

"I'm willing to do anything, Gilly. I'll retain this form during intimacy, I promise. I'll wear whatever you want me to wear and say what you want me to say. Please, husband. Please. I want to be a mother so desperately."

"My god," he sneered. "You think a vile creature like you ought to breed? Are you mad?"

Her sharp intake of breath pierced the cold night air. "You would deny me motherhood? Do you hate me that much?"

"I'm repulsed by you, and I certainly don't want my children to be anything like you. I'd rather the Gillingham line die out than be tainted by whatever flows through your veins. I'm making it my life's work to see that unnaturals like you become extinct. Do you understand, Harriet?"

Lady Gillingham sobbed loudly.

The curtain was suddenly thrust aside, into Lincoln's face, so that he didn't immediately see who came into the room from the balcony. He stood still as the heavy velvet resettled in time for him to watch Gillingham march out of the room, his walking stick not even touching the floor. A moment later, Lady Gillingham followed, a handkerchief dabbing at her nose. Her gown was of a style that revealed her bare shoulders, yet she didn't shiver or look at all cold.

Like her husband, she didn't notice Lincoln standing silently in the shadows at the edge of the curtain. After a deep sigh, she too left the room, as poised and elegant as a lady of her station ought to be. Yet according to her husband, she was disgusting, unnatural—inhuman, even.

So if Lady Gillingham wasn't human, what was she?

* * *

"HER NAME ISN'T in the ministry files." Lincoln threw his jacket on the bed and loosened his tie. The damn thing had felt like a noose for at least the last hour as he'd warred between leaving the ball and staying longer to learn more. In the end, he'd left when Lady Vickers announced she wanted to retire. Apparently she'd won far too much at cards and nobody wanted to play against her anymore. She had also overheard a thing or two about her son that she hadn't liked.

When she'd confronted Seth, he'd simply shrugged broad shoulders and said, "The apple doesn't fall far from the tree."

"Want us to check again, sir?" Gus asked. "Per'aps she's under her maiden name."

"She isn't." Lincoln tossed his shirt onto the clothes piling up on the bed.

With a sigh, Seth straightened them like a fussy valet. "How do you know?"

"I know every name in our files by heart."

Seth grunted. "Why doesn't that surprise me?"

"Are you sure you overheard Gillingham refuse his wife's advances?" Gus asked. "Seems strange to me. She's a pretty little thing. Can't imagine any fellow not wantin' her in his bed."

Lincoln glared at him. "You doubt me?"

"Er, no."

"So what do you think she is?" Seth asked.

Lincoln pulled his black shirt over his head. "I don't know, but I intend to find out."

"You're going out?" Seth nodded at Lincoln's black shirt and the black woolen waistcoat. "Now? But it's miserable out there."

"I'm going to see what I can learn about her."

"By watching her sleep? That's not normal."

"My methods have never worried you before." Lincoln needed to know if she was the reason Gillingham hated supernaturals, perhaps enough to kill them. Something Gillingham had said to his wife on the balcony haunted Lincoln—he'd discovered her secret back in the summer. Charlie's existence had come to their attention in the summer. Could the two facts be linked? Could the discovery of Lady Gillingham's "true form" have led to him wanting to rid the world of all supernaturals?

"I've never voiced my opinion before." Seth crossed his arms. "I no longer feel like holding back. Is that a problem for you, *sir*?"

"Not as long as you don't have a problem with me ignoring you."

Gus gave a grudging laugh but it quickly died when Seth glared at him.

Lincoln pulled on his leather gloves with reinforced knuckles and slipped into his jacket and boots. He slid a knife down each boot and another into the waistband of his pants. He gave his men a nod and moved past them to the door.

"Her bedroom is the third window from the right, third level," Seth said.

Lincoln stopped. "You've been intimate with her?"

Seth shrugged one shoulder. "She's pretty and her husband wasn't paying her any attention. She needed…relief."

Gus scratched his neck. It was still damp from driving through the rain. "Did you notice anything about her? Did she…you know…act like a human woman does when she's…um…?"

"You mean did she cry out my name in ecstasy, bunch the sheets in her fists, and arch her back as her body shuddered?" Seth gave him a smug look. "Yes, she did all of that, and more.

She acted as every other normal woman acts when I'm with her."

Gus rolled his eyes. "Want me to drive you, sir?"

"I'll walk," Lincoln said.

"But it'll take an age to get back to Mayfair."

"Not if I take the short route."

"What short route?"

"Over the roofs." His rooftop escape from O'Neill's place had been exhilarating. Tonight would be slipperier, but that would serve to keep Lincoln alert and his mind focused. He *needed* to focus.

* * *

LINCOLN SLID up the window sash and listened to the even breathing of a slumbering person. She was loud for a young woman, and the dark lump in the bed was larger than he expected. Perhaps this wasn't Lady Gillingham's room after all, but that of her husband.

He removed his boots before climbing down from the sill and stepping silently on the floor. The breathing stopped. The lump moved. As silent as he'd been, she'd heard him—or sensed him.

She sat up. Turned toward him.

Fuck!

He stepped backward, smacking into the wall with a thump, like an amateur. His heartbeat quickened. The light may be low, but there was enough to see that the...thing sitting up in bed didn't have a woman's shape. It was large, thick, and covered with hair or fur.

"Who is it?" said a voice that matched Lady Gillingham's. "Who's there?"

For all his speed and agility, Lincoln wasn't fast enough. The creature—woman—leapt out of bed and wrapped its

77

massive paws around his throat before he could move or utter a sound.

He struggled, kicked out, and batted the wolf-like chest with his fists. He tried to shove off the paws, but they were too tight, the grip too strong. His throat felt like it was being crushed. Blackness rimmed his vision. He felt himself slipping away into oblivion, a pair of yellow inhuman eyes watching as the last breath left his body.

CHAPTER 6

*E*yes. Gouge the eyes.

The thought flittered through Lincoln's mind. He reached up and dug his fingers into the creature's face.

It let him go and stepped back, out of reach. He should have gone after it, but all he could manage was great gasps of air. Every breath burned his raw throat, but the first swallow hurt more. It felt like he was trying to get a football down.

"You!" The voice was Lady Gillingham's feminine one. He glanced up to see her standing rigid before him, hands on hips, her nightgown barely covering womanly curves. She was pretty, young, and the only visible hair was that on her head, tied into a neat braid that drooped over her shoulder. "What are you doing here, Mr. Fitzroy?" She sounded outraged, appalled, and not at all scared. An ordinary woman would be terrified to wake up to a man in her room. "Well? Answer me."

He swallowed again. A little better this time. The ball had shrunk to cricket size. "I came to see what you are." There was no point pretending otherwise. Civility wasn't in his nature, and they were beyond that anyway. "You're not human."

Her hands slipped off her hips to her sides, but he couldn't see her expression in the dark. "You already know what I am."

"No, I do not."

"I don't understand. Gilly told me all about the ministry when he discovered me in...that form. He said that I have been recorded along with other supernaturals in your files. I assume he was trying to intimidate me, but I didn't mind. I think what you do is a fine thing, and quite necessary."

He indicated a candlestick on her bedside table. "May I?"

"Oh, yes, of course. You cannot see me too well." She handed him a box of matches and he lit the candle.

"You can see me?" he asked.

"My vision is excellent, even in the dark."

"As is your hearing." He held up the candle. Light flickered across the smooth skin of her face, and showed her to be frowning. "Or was it another sense by which you detected me?"

"Hearing at first, and then smell." The frown deepened. "Didn't Gilly give you all the details?"

"He has told me nothing about you. Your...alternate form has come as a surprise to me." More like a shock. He must have hidden it well if she couldn't see it.

She sat on the bed suddenly and folded her hands in her lap. She hadn't reached for a wrap or other garment to cover her thin nightgown. As with earlier on the balcony, it appeared the cold didn't affect her. "I don't understand. Why would Gilly tell me he told you when he hadn't?"

Shame. Pride. Lincoln could think of a number of reasons, but he wasn't sure which would be the driving force behind Gillingham's lie. Nor did he care. "You will have to ask him."

She snorted softly. "He won't tell me." Her shoulders slumped and she studied her hands in her lap. "He rarely talks to me at all, these days."

He didn't come near her for intimacy, either, it seemed. "What are you, madam?"

She glanced up. "You don't know? Even with all your experience?"

"I've never come across anyone like you before."

"Oh. I was hoping you could tell me. I have no name for what I am. My father never told me, you see, and now he's gone."

"Did you inherit this...magic from him?"

She nodded. "My father could change form too. When I was young, he told me to always use my human shape and not tell a soul about the other. Apparently he never told my mother, but I don't know how she reacted when she first saw me change. She died when I was quite young, so I'll never know. Lately, I've wondered if seeing me become a monster killed her."

"You're not a monster."

Her head snapped up. Her eyes filled with tears. What had he said? Why did she want to cry? "You don't think so?" she whispered.

"As soon as you recognized me, you let me go. A monster would have killed me, especially after I witnessed you in that form. You haven't killed your husband either." Although she must have wanted to, on occasion. God knew Lincoln wanted to—frequently.

"I suppose."

"Did he find out by accident?"

She nodded. "He came in here one night to...see me. I was asleep. When I sleep, I can't control which form I take." Her fingers twisted and locked together. "He was horrified and screamed the place down."

Lincoln didn't doubt it.

"I shifted shape to this one immediately, but it took quite some time to calm him. His screaming woke the servants, and I had to send them away before I could explain to him. He hasn't been the same since. He won't even look at me and he refuses to…visit me now."

"When did this happen?"

"Late summer. He'd been out drinking at his club. I hoped he would wake up in the morning and forget what he'd seen, or perhaps attribute it to his inebriated state. Unfortunately, he did not." She sighed and gave him a flat smile. "I have come to accept his disgust and fear of me. He won't divorce me because he has no grounds, unless he tells everyone what I truly am. He's too proud to do that. Besides, no one would believe him. So he's stuck with me."

"And you with him." Lincoln thought she'd got the rougher end of the bargain.

Her face fell. She thrust out her lower lip in a pout. "If he would get me with child, I would be quite happy."

Lincoln didn't want to hear about her domestic situation. He already knew more than he cared to know. "There are no records of you in the ministry archives, or of anyone who can become an animal like you."

"So Gilly didn't tell a soul. That's something, at least."

"I will record you in our files, but I will not announce it, if you prefer. The other committee members don't need to know, only my employees. Nor will I tell your husband about this conversation, and I ask that you don't inform him either. It's best if he doesn't know."

"Of course. He wouldn't understand. Thank you for your consideration, Mr. Fitzroy. I don't mind you creating a file about me. I quite like the idea of being recorded for posterity. I'm unique, you say?"

"As far as I am aware, but I'm beginning to think our

records are woefully incomplete." He indicated the space on the bed beside her and she nodded. He sat. "May I ask you some questions about yourself?"

"Of course." Her smile was a little wobbly. "It'll be nice to talk to someone about it. Someone who isn't afraid of me, or disgusted, that is."

After half an hour, he'd learned that she could shift between her human and animal states with ease and at will; that she had animal-like hearing, vision and smell. She was a female in her other form too, and her father had told her that she should be capable of bearing children, and they would likely have some of her characteristics, although to a lesser degree. Her father had been faster and stronger than her, and his senses more acute. He had never told her why he'd been born like that, or which parent he'd inherited it from. His parents had died when he was young, so it was possible they'd never told him.

"Thank you," Lincoln said, rising. "I appreciate your honesty. And not choking me to death."

She laughed softly. "I must learn to control that urge. I forget my own strength. I'd hate to throttle a burglar."

He put his boots back on and climbed onto the sill. "Goodnight, madam."

"Would you prefer to go out through the front door?" she asked.

"This is quieter."

"It's a long way down. You'll die if you fall."

"Then I won't fall."

She laughed again. "Are you sure you're not part animal too? Perhaps a monkey?"

"Not that I am aware." He swung his legs through the window and scrambled up the pipe running along the wall.

"Goodnight," she whispered.

He glanced down when he reached the roofline. She

waved up at him from the window, then went inside and drew down the sash. He swung himself up onto the roof and headed back across the city. He paused in Clerkenwell and climbed down to street level. Charlie's gang had lived in one of the dilapidated houses, the entrance to their den almost hidden from view. Lincoln had asked his contacts where to find it, back when he'd been searching for her in the summer. It had cost him a considerable sum to the right people. Few had known where the "boy" who'd escaped from Highgate Police Station lived.

He shucked off his coat, folded it, and placed it beside the boarded up hole in the wall. He knocked on the boards then leaped onto the crate and used the eaves to propel himself up to the neighboring roof. A head poked through the entrance, looked left then right, but not up. A hand darted out, grabbed the coat and disappeared back inside.

Lincoln headed home.

THERE WERE no records of Lady Gillingham's father's birth in the General Registry Office. That didn't mean one didn't exist in another parish outside London, but since she hadn't known where he'd come from, it would be impossible to learn more about him.

Right now, it didn't matter. It wouldn't help Lincoln locate the killer. What he needed to know was whether Gillingham was outraged enough by his wife's true form that he would kill other supernaturals. He had already sent Gus out to track the baron's movements, and Seth would relieve him later. They weren't to let him out of their sights.

Seth deposited Lincoln at the front of the house and continued on to the coach house. Doyle took Lincoln's hat and coat.

"There's a fellow to see you, sir." The look of disgust on Doyle's face told Lincoln he'd likely find this fellow in the service area, not the parlor. "He refused to give his name, but he's rather scruffy and thinks he's a lark. Cook almost chased him off with his meat cleaver and one of his frightening glares, but I convinced him to stay."

It sounded like Billy the Bolter. "Thank you. Send him into the library."

Lincoln headed there himself and poured a brandy. Billy swaggered to the doorway then stopped, cap in hand. His jaw dropped as he took in the rich velvet curtains, the walls of books and the heavy furniture that Doyle had polished to a high sheen.

"Nice digs." Billy continued into the room, his swagger not quite as pronounced.

Lincoln handed him the glass. "Well?"

"Right to it, then, eh?" Billy sniffed the brandy then drank the lot. He wiped his sleeve across his mouth and held the glass out for a refill. Lincoln obliged, and Billy drank that too. "Got me money?"

"I'll pay you if your information is worthwhile."

Billy considered this. With a nod, he said, "I heard something 'round the traps about the gunman. I think I know who he is."

"Go on."

"After you and me spoke last time, I got it in my head to ask around here and there. All quiet, like. Just some as I could trust." He held up his finger and smiled a yellow-toothed smile. "I ain't stupid."

Did the man expect affirmation? "Go on."

"My sister told me 'bout a bloke who's been hangin' round Osborne Street, where some doxies do business. She ain't a street worker, but she got some friends who are. Well, one of 'em said a fellow's been splashing the ready 'round to all the girls in the last week. He's been there before, but never had no money until now. My sister's friend asked him where he got the ready from, and he said it were a secret but it involved his barker. She didn't believe he had one, so he showed it to her."

"She saw his gun?"

"Aye, she swears she did. He reckons he stole it from some toff, and ever since then, he put word out he'd use it for the right price."

"Do you know this fellow?"

"I know *of* him. Name's Jack Daley, and he's a mean blighter. He'd kill a man, sure enough, if he wronged him."

"Or was paid?"

"Aye."

"Do you know where I can find him?" Lincoln asked.

"He lives in a lodging house on Flower and Dean Street. Don't know which one."

"Anything else?"

"Aye. When you get 'im, don't tell 'im how you found 'im."

"That goes without saying."

"No, it don't." Billy turned serious. "He'd hurt me sister and her friend bad if he knew they ratted. He don't need more reason than that to slash their throats."

Lincoln fetched Billy some money and told him to pass some on to his sister and her friend. He almost fetched some clothes that Charlie had left behind, but decided against it. That would require him to enter her room.

"Thank you, sir. Been good doin' business with you again." Billy tugged on his forelock and left through the front door as Doyle looked on disapprovingly.

"Would you like luncheon, sir?" Doyle asked after shutting the door.

"Bring something to my rooms. And send Seth in when he's finished outside."

Lincoln made his way upstairs only to be accosted by Lady Vickers on the landing. She blocked his path when he tried to move around her. He should have taken the service stairs.

"I would like to know if I'm available to callers this afternoon," she said with an incline of her chin. She looked like a taller version of the queen today, dressed in deep black with a black lace cap over her hair. He suspected that was to hide the poor job her new maid did of arranging it. Some of the strands had already come loose.

"I don't care if you receive callers or not," Lincoln said.

He tried to move but once again, she blocked his way. "And you, Mr. Fitzroy? Will you be home to callers?"

"I don't have any. Those who do visit are used to me rarely being home."

"I think today will be different."

"I doubt it."

She gave him a small smile that seemed to indicate she knew something that he did not. "Did you not notice the sensation your presence caused last night?"

He noticed Julia's attentions, and the gazes of Miss Overton and her mother, but that hardly constituted a sensation. "I think you're mistaken."

"Oh no, Mr. Fitzroy. I am never mistaken when it comes to sensations. And you, sir, are one. Apparently you rarely go to balls or parties, and that makes you a curious figure. An air of mystery is very desirable in a gentleman, particularly a wealthy one. Your unknown lineage will not hold you back when it comes to the ladies, but some of their fathers are more cautious."

He held up his hands. "I'm not on the market."

She made a scoffing noise through her nose. "Nonsense. All unwed gentlemen are on the market. We can use this new intrigue to our advantage."

"We?"

She clicked her tongue. "Must I spell it out to you?"

"Yes."

She sighed. "Honestly, for a clever man, you're very stupid. Let me explain it in simple terms. Now that you have made an appearance in society, the eligible girls have gone wild. This goes doubly for my son, of course, since he's titled. Ordinarily, two handsome, interesting bachelors would cause a problem. I'm not sure how Marjory Wadsworth did it. She has twin sons, you know."

"And?"

"Don't talk, just listen. Usually, the best candidate will win the best girl, and of course, that would be Seth since he's so agreeable. I am sorry to be blunt, Mr. Fitzroy, but I'm sure it won't shock you to learn that some girls are as afraid of you as they are intrigued by you."

"I'm not shocked."

"But since Seth's reputation is a little...tarnished, your star has risen somewhat, and I would consider you both even in the race. The girls only need to choose between a wealthy gentleman—yourself—or a titled one. That separates the girls into two camps quite neatly—those who need to marry money and those who can afford to fish around for an agreeable titled gentleman. Forget that simpering Miss Overton. I don't know what Julia is thinking. She would be more appropriate for my Seth, although I can think of better. You, on the other hand, would be suited to the Chester girl. Her father's a viscount, no less, and the estate is in ruin. He's desperate to marry her off. She tends to squint, and I suspect she needs glasses, but you shouldn't let that bother you. She's quite spirited and has a strong will, which Seth tells me is your sort—"

"Enough! I do not want a wife."

"But you need one. Besides, you had a fiancée..."

"And now I don't." He must have looked quite fierce because Lady Vickers swayed backward, away from him, and she didn't seem like the sort of woman to intimidate easily. "I am not home to callers today or any other day."

"I see. What about my son?"

"He can marry whomever he wants, but this afternoon, he has work to do for me." He tried to move around her again, but she once more blocked his path. It wouldn't be easy to pick her up and forcibly move her, as he did with Charlie when she stood in his way, but he would try if it became necessary.

"Seth is not your servant," she said stiffly.

"I beg to differ. Excuse me, madam."

She puffed out her chest, as if trying to make herself larger. "He is Lord Vickers, thank you very much."

"You and your son are here under my roof because I allow it. I can throw you out, if I wish."

Her hand fluttered at her chest and tears pooled in her eyes. It was Lincoln, however, who took a step back. Perhaps he'd gone too far. Sometimes he forgot that female sensibilities were more delicate. It occurred to him that Charlie would have picked up her skirts and marched right past him if he'd spoken to her like that. She probably would have left Lichfield then and there to prove a point.

"You're being deliberately difficult," Lady Vickers said quietly. "I don't like it."

He drew in a breath to quell his rising temper. This woman didn't deserve his ire. "I am merely pointing out that this is my house and your son is employed by me. He is not at liberty to do as he pleases." He held up his hand again. "If he wants to be paid, that is."

She pulled a face. "There is no need to rub it in. I am well aware of our reduced circumstances."

"Then kindly see to your visitors yourself. Seth and I will not be home."

"Very well." She thrust out that very determined chin again and Lincoln braced himself. She hadn't given up yet. "But I should warn you that you are not as in command here as you think you are."

"I pay everyone's wages. I am in complete control."

She waved a hand. "Tosh. You may pay them, but that doesn't give you control. When I look at you, all I see is a man running hither and thither, and treating his friends like they're staff."

"They are staff," he growled.

"Seth is not." She stated it as if it were a fact, without malice or pomposity. "He's your friend, and he's trying to help you, but you're making it impossible for him and that other fellow. You're too busy dashing off chasing shadows and trying *not* to look in at yourself."

He stiffened. If he simply used brute strength, he could barrel past her. He doubted that would silence her, however. She'd probably shout her opinion at him until she was hoarse.

Her face softened and her eyes turned gentle. He didn't know her well, but the change in her worried him. He preferred her vitriol to her pity. "You're scared of what you'll see," she said. "That's why you don't want to look."

The blood chugged sluggishly through his veins. His extremities turned cold and he curled his fingers into fists to warm them. "I know what I'll see," he told her. A cold, dead heart. Gus had told him so.

"It doesn't have to be like this. Seth said you changed with her."

"This is how I am and how I must be." His jaw hurt to speak. Everything hurt. "People depend upon me. The country depends on me. I have ministry affairs to see to, and introspection is a waste of time and energy that could be spent working."

Most people would back away from him now, seeing the signs of his temper rising. But not Lady Vickers, damn her. She was like Charlie in that respect. "Introspection is how we become better people, and how we learn from our mistakes," she said.

"I don't make mistakes."

"From what I've seen and heard, you've made a very big one, and you know it. *That's* why you don't like to be introspective. Looking inward will show you that you failed."

"I have not failed."

To his surprise, she lowered her gaze and stepped aside. Not quickly or with shaking hands, but because she had no more to say to him. He stalked past her and tried to dampen his temper, but he hadn't succeeded by the time he slammed his door. He shed his day clothes and put on the ones he used for when he wanted to walk through the slums unnoticed.

By the time he tied the gray cloth around his neck, he'd decided Lady Vickers was a crackpot and meddler. She wasn't worth wasting his time on. He had more important business to tend do. Ministry business.

* * *

SETH AND LINCOLN stopped at the mews behind Gillingham's house to pick up Gus. "Nothing to report," he told Lincoln as he settled on the seat opposite. "He ain't been out yet today. So where we goin'?"

"Flower and Dean Street."

Gus stroked the scar stretching from his cheek to the corner of his eye. "Last time we went to them parts, the brougham almost got stolen."

"We'll leave it at the Pig and Whistle's stables. The ostler

91

knows me. It's not much of a walk from there." Lincoln told him everything Billy the Bolter had reported and then outlined his plan.

"Thank you, sir," Gus said at the end.

"For what?"

"For tellin' me. Time was, you wouldn't have said nothin' about the whole plan, just my part."

Lincoln turned to the window and tried to think back, but it felt like another life, another century. He wasn't that same man anymore. The revelation was like a bolt of lightning, shocking him to his core.

He'd barely recovered by the time they arrived at the Pig and Whistle. He paid the hunchbacked ostler to mind the horses and coach, then headed to Flower and Dean Street with Gus and Seth. This part of Whitechapel was infamous for the violent Ripper murders, and a sense of unease and mistrust flowed from the passersby, hitting his senses with force.

Lincoln felt conspicuous, even though he'd gone to some trouble to blend in with the working class men. Perhaps it was because most of those men were at work in the early afternoon, not wandering around the streets in a pack of three. Lincoln regretted not waiting for darkness, when the men were heading home from their jobs at the factories. He worked better in the dark too.

But he'd been too impatient to wait. If Billy's information proved true, then Lincoln could be close to catching the gunman as well the man who hired him. Waiting would allow the gunman to escape.

"I hate this place," Gus hissed. He hunched into his great coat, but still shivered. "Feels like I'm bein' sized for me boots."

"Not even the poorest will want your stinking footwear."

Seth's teasing was half-hearted, as he too kept a wary eye on the hollow-eyed children and their gin-soaked mothers.

They passed a group of thick-set men huddled around a low fire burning in a brazier. One man drank from a bottle while his friends rubbed gloveless hands together and laughed over something. Others stood a little further away, gazing enviously at the fire but not approaching.

"Should we ask them?" Seth said.

"No." Lincoln knew a group of thugs when he saw it. There were easier targets who would be more deserving of a few coins.

Gus tripped over the feet of an elderly man sitting on a doorstep. His head remained resting against the door, his mouth ajar. Lincoln couldn't be certain if he was asleep or dead.

A girl stumbled out of the shadows, a ragged shawl bunched at her chest instead of wrapped around her thin shoulders. Stringy brown hair fell from a cap that had probably once been white but was now gray and torn. Her face was mostly gray too. The only color came from the smudges of red under her sunken eyes and the sores on her lips.

"Please, sirs. I'll do whatever you want for some ready." She let go of the shawl and held out her dirty palm. The shawl fell away to reveal a sleeping baby. The baby stirred with the sudden brush of cold air on soft skin. Unlike the girl, the baby looked healthy.

Both Seth and Gus reached for their pockets but Lincoln stopped them with a raise of his hand. "Do you know where we can find Jack Daley?" he asked her.

A spark of fear momentarily gave her eyes some life. She looked left and right, then backed away. She shook her head.

Lincoln removed a pouch stuffed with coin from his inside coat pocket. "All of this and my coat if you tell me where to find him."

For a moment, he thought her fear would override her desperation, but then she stepped forward. "He lives in the tall brown house on Flower and Dean," she whispered. "Two from the corner. Old Mrs. Fenton is the landlady." She blinked at Lincoln then tentatively held out her hand again.

He gave her the pouch and she quickly tucked it back inside the shawl with the baby. "How old are you?" he asked.

"Thirteen."

Both Seth and Gus muttered under their breath. "The baby's father?" Seth asked.

"Dead. Our mother too."

"You're not the mother?"

"He's me brother." She blinked dry eyes and kissed the top of the baby's head. "I'm all he's got now, and he's all I got."

Lincoln shucked off his coat and draped it around her shoulders. He must remember to ask Doyle to get more made.

"You don't want nothing else, sir?" she asked.

Lincoln shook his head. He should walk away, but for some reason he couldn't. What was wrong with him?

Gus laid a hand on the girl's shoulder. She shrank back. "Do you know how to get to Seven Dials from here?" he asked.

She nodded quickly.

"Find Broker Row and ask for Mary Sullivan. Tell her Gus sent you. She'll take care of you and your brother."

"Thank you, sir." She clutched the baby tighter to her breast and hurried away.

"We can't save them all," Seth said, as they moved off toward Flower and Dean Street.

Lincoln made no comment. He found it easier not to dwell on such things, but it was difficult to dismiss the girl and her baby brother from his mind. Sending Gus to his great aunt's house later to see if the girl arrived safely was a pointless exercise, yet he resolved to do it.

Old Mrs. Fenton's lodging house was a palace compared to the other terraces on Flower and Dean. It was a full story taller and the arched windows gave it a grandeur that not even the peeling paint and grimy stones destroyed. It even had a balcony on the second level. The rest of Flower and Dean was a confused collection of short and tall buildings, some brick, some wood, but few stone. Smoke drifted from the chimney of Mrs. Fenton's house, but not the others.

Lincoln set Gus on watch out the front while he and Seth headed down the nearest lane and through an archway to the large courtyard at the back of the properties. The buildings surrounding the courtyard were in such poor state that a strong breeze might have knocked them over. The dense, still air reeked of feces and something rotting.

A man exited from the back of Mrs. Fenton's house and pissed on the slick cobbles. He swayed on his feet and didn't look up. If he had, he would have spotted Seth and Lincoln.

When the man tucked himself back into his trousers, his elbow nudged aside his coat to reveal the handle of a pistol.

Lincoln signaled Seth to fetch Gus.

"You're going to wait for us to return before you approach him, aren't you?" Seth whispered.

"Yes."

With a nod of approval, Seth returned down the lane. Not even that movement alerted the man to their presence. He rocked back on his heels, licked his fingers and dragged them through his greasy black hair.

Lincoln stepped out of the shadows. He got to within four steps before the man looked up. "Jack Daley?"

The man reached for his gun, but Lincoln was too fast. He snatched the pistol and pointed it at the man's temple.

"Are you Jack Daley?" he asked again.

"Who wants to know?"

"The person who holds this gun at your head and has no qualms about pulling the trigger."

Daley had a high forehead and a moustache so thin that it looked like an outline of his top lip. His clothes were new and his jaw smooth. He'd recently come into money. He sized up Lincoln with a sneer. "You ain't got the bollocks."

Lincoln shot him in the foot.

Daley screamed and crumpled to the ground. A woman came to the door, gasped, and hurried back inside. The tumbling of the heavy lock was almost as loud as Daley's cries.

"It's dangerous to keep your weapon loaded," Lincoln told him.

Daley's only response was to change from screaming to whimpering. Lincoln aimed the pistol at his other foot.

"Unless you want me to make you a cripple, you'll answer my questions. Are you Jack Daley?"

"Aye! Bloody hell, man, what'd you shoot me for?"

"I know what you've done to the people in these parts. I know they fear you. Perhaps now they'll hear you limping toward them in time to get away."

Lincoln heard Seth and Gus's running footsteps before they entered the courtyard. "Jesus," Gus muttered, staring at Daley's bloodied boot. "Did you shoot him?"

"He wasn't answering my questions."

"Fair enough, then."

Seth marched up to Lincoln. "You said you would wait."

Lincoln watched his men grab Daley and haul him up to stand on his one good foot. "I lied."

Seth rolled his eyes. "Has he confessed?"

"To what?" Daley spat. He tried to pull away but Seth and Gus held him too tightly and his foot must have pained him. He gave up with a wince and whimper. "What do you want?"

"I want to know who hired you to kill Patrick O'Neill," Lincoln said.

Daley went even paler. "You the pigs?"

"The police don't shoot suspects. They waste time with protocol. I prefer to get my answers quickly. Did you kill Patrick O'Neill?"

"No."

Lincoln cocked the pistol.

"Don't shoot!" Daley squeezed his eyes shut. His moustache almost disappeared up his nostrils. When the gun didn't go off, he cracked open one eye. "Is it me you want or the man who hired me?"

"You're not important to me."

Daley blew out a breath and stood a little straighter. "It were a blood nut what paid me. He told me who to shoot and where to find him. I didn't know it was the circus strongman, did I? Are you with them? Are you one of them circus freaks?"

"Do you know the redheaded man's name?"

"No, but I know what he really looks like and he ain't no true blood nut. Nor a toff, neither." His lips curled into a vicious smile. "He wore a disguise. He's got short, brown hair and don't need the glasses he wore when I met him."

"Where can I find him?"

He shrugged.

Lincoln pointed the gun at his head and Daley shut his eyes again and tried to shrink away. "You must have followed him to see him remove his disguise," Lincoln said. "Tell me where I can find him."

Daley went to shift his weight only to receive a rude reminder of his injury. He grunted in pain. A waxy sheen covered his pale face.

Lincoln pressed the barrel of the gun harder into Daley's temple. He was so close to victory he could taste it, but he had to be careful not to show how much he needed this information. "If you remain silent much longer, I'll kill you. If you tell me where to find this man, I'll let you go and you can leave London alive. That's your choice. You have three seconds in which to make it. One. Two."

"All right!" Daley screwed up his face. Despite the cold, sweat beaded at his hairline. "I saw how much ready he carried on him, so I thought I could relieve him of some of it. To give to the poor, see."

Gus snorted. "We ain't stupid."

Daley cleared his throat. "I followed his coach to Kensington. It left him at the Queens Arms, and he walked down the mews. I followed. When he thought no one was watching, he removed his wig, glasses and some padding round his middle under his clothes and stored them at the back of one of the stables. I was so surprised I forgot why I followed him. By the time I remembered, he were climbing the ladder to the rooms above."

"Not the main house?"

"No. I thought he'd come down again, but he didn't. His lamp went out and that were it. No one stirred again 'til morning."

"You stayed the whole night?"

"Aye. I were curious, see. I asked the stable lad who the cove was, and he said Mr. Thomas Rampling."

"Is he a servant?"

"No, just a cove that knows the coachman."

"Did he have anything to do with the household?"

"Don't know. I didn't ask."

"Did you ask if he'd had contact with others aside from the stable staff?"

"Why would I?"

"Who did he pay you to kill next?"

"A woman named Metzger. Lives at forty-four Brick Lane, Spitalfields."

Lincoln lowered the gun. The name was familiar. She also had a file in the archives.

Daley's tongue darted out and he licked his lips. "Who're you? Why'd you want to know all this?"

Lincoln nodded at Seth and Gus to let Daley go then walked away. He didn't look back, but he heard Daley shout for Mrs. Fenton to unlock the door.

"Gus, find a policeman and tell him Jack Daley shot Patrick O'Neill," he said. "If by any chance he's not caught, find the Metzger woman and get her to safety." He tucked the gun into the waistband of his trousers and covered it with his jacket. He might need it again.

CHAPTER 7

"*J*ain't seen him all day." The stable boy leaned on his broom and shrugged lanky shoulders, as if he wasn't surprised by this event. "He comes back late and sometimes goes out again at night."

"Why is Rampling staying here?" Lincoln asked. "Does he know the master of the house?"

"He's cousin to the coachman, also a Rampling. John Rampling." He nodded at the glossy black carriage, where a pair of boot soles could be seen in the window.

Lincoln thanked the lad and opened the cabin door. The boots dropped, and the fellow wearing them sprang upright, his eyes wide. When he saw it wasn't his master, he yawned and lay down again.

"What'd you want?" he growled.

"I want to ask you about your cousin, Thomas Rampling," Lincoln said. "What business is he conducting?"

"No business." The coachman folded his arms over his chest. "He's a drifter, just comes and goes."

"Do you know when he'll be back?"

"Nope."

The rumble of wheels and click clack of hooves on cobbles announced the arrival of another vehicle. The stable lad went out to greet it, but John Rampling didn't stir. Lincoln was about to question him further, but a shout from the boy interrupted him.

"Mr. Rampling! Mr. Rampling, come quick! It's your cousin."

Rampling stretched and sat up again. "What is it now?"

The boy swallowed. "He's dead."

The coachman blinked. "Can't be. I only saw him last night."

The lad glanced over his shoulder at the cart that had stopped behind Lincoln's coach. A police constable stood beside it, squinting into the shadows of the coach house.

Lincoln felt everything inside him tighten into a ball. His heart sank. Every time he got closer to getting answers, the trail went cold. The two grave robbers, Captain Jasper, the man who'd killed Drinkwater and Brumley...all died after their identities and secrets were uncovered by the ministry. Their deaths weren't coincidences, and certainly weren't accidents. Someone was a step ahead of Lincoln—and that infuriated him.

Seth was first out of the coach house, followed by Rampling and Lincoln. "This is John Rampling," Seth said when the coachman simply stood at the end of the cart and stared at the lump beneath the gray blanket.

The constable nodded a greeting but got none in return. "He was pulled out of the river this morning," he said as he lifted the blanket.

The bloated face of the dead man was clear evidence of how he'd died. If that wasn't enough, his clothes and hair were still wet.

The coachman gagged then threw up on the cobbles. The

policeman went to cover the deceased again, but Lincoln stopped him. He inspected the victim's face.

"Are there any marks on him?" he asked.

"A cut on the back of his head," the constable said. "He was probably standing on a pier when he lost his footing, hit his head and got knocked out." He shrugged. "Slipped into the water and drowned, is my guess."

"Oh God," the coachman moaned. "I can't believe it. Tom's gone."

"We found a note on him addressed to these mews so came here directly. Can you confirm that this is your cousin, Mr. Thomas Rampling?"

John Rampling nodded. "Where are you taking him?"

"Mortuary in Chelsea."

"Who was the note from?" Lincoln asked.

The constable settled his feet apart and glared at Lincoln. "Who're you in relation to the deceased?"

Lincoln was still considering the most efficient method to relieve the constable of the note when Seth said, "Mr. Rampling would like to see it."

The constable glanced at the coachman who simply stared at his cousin's body, oblivious to the attention. The constable waited. After a nudge from Seth, Lincoln handed the policeman three shillings. The constable removed the note from the deceased's pocket. He handed it to Rampling, but when he didn't move to take it, passed it to Lincoln.

The soggy card was thick, like a gentleman's calling card. It bore no signature or indication as to who'd sent it. The barely legible words read: "Shadwell Dock Stairs. Midnight." Lincoln passed it back to the constable.

The policeman leapt onto the back of the cart and ordered the driver to exit the mews. Once he was out of sight, Rampling crouched down and ran both hands through his hair. Lincoln felt like doing the same.

"Do you know who wrote that note?" Lincoln asked him.

Rampling wiped the back of his hand across his eyes and stood. "Tom never told me his business. I knew he was doing some work for someone that involved wearing disguises from time to time, but I never asked what he was doing. God," he moaned. "I have to write to his mother."

Seth clapped him on the shoulder. "What was his middle name?"

Lincoln sucked in a breath. He glared at Seth, but Seth wasn't looking his way.

"James," Rampling said. "Why?"

"No particular reason."

Rampling looked up. "You didn't tell me why you came looking for Thomas."

"It no longer matters," Seth said, far more cheerfully than was appropriate considering the circumstances. He gathered the reins for Lincoln's horse and climbed onto the driver's seat. Instead of sitting in the cabin, Lincoln got up beside him.

"Aren't you going to say something?" Seth asked as they passed the Queen's Arms.

"No," Lincoln said.

"Not even to tell me there was no point getting the dead man's middle name because Charlie's not here to call his spirit back?"

Lincoln didn't respond. Hopefully his lack of communication would shut Seth up. Unfortunately, it seemed to have the opposite effect.

"If she was here, she could summon the spirit and find out who hired Rampling to hire Jack Daley," he went on. "You do know that Rampling was most likely killed because he could identify the man who hired him, don't you?"

Captain Jasper too, although Lincoln hadn't connected his death to the current murders until recently. He could have asked her to raise Jasper, but using her necromancy like that had felt wrong, particularly when he was warning her *not* to use it.

The whip of the icy wind slapped Lincoln's cheeks, and it began raining as they passed through Camden Town. Each drop pelted down from the dense mass of cloud overhead like sharp shards of glass. Seth flipped up his hood but Lincoln had given his coat to the girl in Flower and Dean Street. He took over the reins and urged the horse to go faster.

"Careful!" Seth grabbed onto the side rail as they took a sharp corner without slowing.

Lincoln didn't slow down until they reached Lichfield's coach house. Gus was already waiting.

"Did the police catch Daley?" Seth asked as he jumped down.

Gus nodded. "Got him before he even left the lodgin' house. He was screamin' at them about gettin' his foot seen by a doctor."

Lincoln helped Gus unharness the coach then Seth led the horse to the stables. Lincoln and Gus joined him a few minutes later. While they all worked, Seth told Gus about Rampling's demise, including the fact that they could have discovered who'd hired him by now if Charlie was with them.

That was Lincoln's cue to return inside, but Gus stopped him with a growl, "If you don't want her back for your own good, then what about the greater good? She's useful."

"She's not a tool." Lincoln had snapped out the words before he could check himself.

"She ain't a parcel to be sent across the country neither!"

Seth laid a hand on Gus's shoulder. He half-raised his other hand in a calming gesture, as if he were approaching a wild horse. "Let me handle this," he muttered.

Had they discussed this between them? It wouldn't surprise Lincoln if they had. They'd taken Charlie's departure badly and neither seemed the same since. They'd certainly changed their attitude toward Lincoln. Sometimes he was surprised they still worked for him. Part of him wondered if they remained because they expected him to fetch Charlie back, or if they thought they could manipulate him into doing so.

He wasn't going to let them push him. In fact, why discuss it at all? He'd made his decision. He didn't care what they thought.

He strode out of the coach house. The rain pummeled him again and formed puddles in the low lying corner of the courtyard. He was already wet through to the bone and a few more drops didn't matter.

"You have to bring her home," Seth shouted. He was closer than Lincoln expected.

He turned to see they'd both followed him and stood in the courtyard as soaked as he was. "Go inside," he told them. "Dry off. Neither of you will be of use to me if you become ill."

"Neither of us will be of use if we refuse to work for you!" Gus shouted back.

So it had come to that after all. "Are you leaving my employ?"

Seth once again held up his hands in a placating gesture. Rain dripped off his hair down his face. He swiped angrily at his eyes. "Can we go inside to discuss this?"

"There's nothing to discuss."

"Bloody hell." Seth shook his head, spraying droplets. "Don't you see that this has affected you?"

That wasn't what Lincoln had expected him to say. "I'm the same as I've always been."

Gus snorted. "No, you're not," Seth said. "You're acting erratically and have been ever since she left."

"You're mistaken."

Gus shook his head. "You don't care about your own safety no more."

Lincoln had never cared. He went to walk away, but Seth's words stopped him.

"No, that's not what I meant. I meant you've lost focus now. Answers that were once easy to obtain have become elusive. Details that were obvious are now less so. You do foolish things that jeopardize your own safety because you're distracted. You thought she was a distraction when she was here, but her absence is doubly so. Isn't it?"

Rain thundered on the tiled roof of the coach house and stables. Drips slid past Lincoln's collar and down his spine, leaving a painfully icy trail in their wake. His men watched him through the veil of rain, their gazes searching, questioning. Hoping. They didn't know for certain. They were only guessing at Lincoln's motives and state of mind.

He clung to that as if it were a buoy.

"You miss her," Seth said, more quietly. "You miss her terribly."

Lincoln squinted up into the sky, ignoring the rain splattering his face. The heavy clouds seemed to blanket the whole world, smothering every breath. He should go inside. He should walk away from his men and not answer them.

But for a reason he couldn't fathom, he wanted to answer. "Yes. I miss her." He tilted his head forward and looked at each of them in turn. He needed to get his next point across. "But it will pass."

They scoffed. Gus shook his head. "You're a fool if you think we believe that," Seth said.

"You're a fool if *you* believe it," Gus added.

Lincoln's face heated. He could feel his temper rising

from the depths of him, bubbling to the surface. "How would you know?"

Neither seemed to think it a question worth answering. But the longer the silence stretched, the more Lincoln realized his question was sincere.

"I owe you much," Seth said, folding his arms up high on his chest and not meeting Lincoln's gaze. "I don't know where I'd be now if it weren't for you. I like working for the ministry."

Lincoln looked to Gus, but his craggy features gave nothing away.

"I don't want to leave," Seth went on. "But I feel I must. I can't work for someone who acts irrationally. And she kept you in check."

"In check how?" Lincoln asked.

"You shot a man in the foot!"

"I didn't kill him."

"You traversed the city over rooftops. In the rain."

"It was a shorter, faster way."

Seth threw his hands in the air. "You try," he said to Gus. "I give up."

Gus blew out a breath. "How can I put it?" He thought a moment then nodded. "I'll be direct with you, sir. If you got rid of Charlie because she got in the way, what will you do with us if we make a mistake?"

"Don't make mistakes and you won't find out."

Seth barked out a humorless laugh.

Gus rubbed his temple. "What if we're no longer useful? Will you shoot us in the foot if we don't do something you ask or do it the wrong way?"

"Or will you kill us?" Seth said, quieter.

Lincoln watched them from beneath damp lashes. Did they think pressuring him would encourage him to bring Charlie home? "If you feel you must go, then go. I won't stop you." He turned and walked to the house. He sensed them following at a distance.

He avoided the kitchen and went through the main part of the house. The salver on the table by the front door overflowed with calling cards. Had Lady Vickers had that many callers, or were some for Lincoln and Seth? His progress up the stairs was deliberately slow, steady, yet he felt like he'd run for miles by the time he shut his door. He shouldn't feel this exhausted after so little exertion. He changed into dry clothes and poured himself a tumbler of brandy, then another and another. It didn't clear his head, only made the fog denser.

If Seth and Gus left, he still had Cook and Doyle. But it wasn't the same. They weren't fighters. Their duties were in the house. And they didn't know how Lincoln worked, not like the others. They just weren't the same, damn them, and Lincoln *wanted* the same. He wanted Seth and Gus at his side, complete with their bickering and bad jokes.

He threw the glass into the fireplace. It shattered, spraying shards over the hearth, the floor, onto the rug, over tables and chairs. He marched over. Glass pierced the soles of his feet. It hurt like the devil and no amount of concentration could deaden the pain. He used to be able to master pain— not eliminate it, just mask it. But now, every cut burned, and soon his feet felt like they were on fire.

He hobbled back to his desk, leaving a trail of bloody footprints behind. He sat down and closed his eyes. Let the pain come. Let it consume him and see if it destroyed him.

And if it didn't?

He would get up in the morning and face the day and every day that came after it. He would bury himself in work to the point where *it* consumed him instead. He would find a way through to the other side.

What he felt now… it couldn't possibly last forever.

* * *

The Metzger woman.

Lincoln awoke with a start. He'd forgotten about the Metzger woman! How could he have been so incompetent?

He set his feet on the floor only to wince as pain spiked through them. He sucked in a breath and blew it out slowly, then sucked in another. He stood. Manageable.

He'd bandaged his feet himself the night before using the medical kit he kept in his study. Hopefully he'd removed all the glass first.

He dressed quickly and edged aside the curtain. Light rimmed another gray, dull horizon. It wasn't raining but it probably would later.

He headed downstairs, avoiding all the creaking floorboards, and outside. His feet stung but so be it. He harnessed a horse to the smaller cabriolet and drove out of the Lichfield estate at speed, heading toward Spitalfields. He easily passed the delivery carts with their yawning drivers and plodding hacks.

Number forty-four A had once been half of a sizable residence but was now a two-up two-down with four windows, set evenly apart, and a green door. A tanned woman with sagging sacks beneath her eyes and deep grooves around her mouth answered his knock. She shrank back when she saw him. Her eyes turned guarded. It was impossible to tell if she was owner of the house or a lodger. She wouldn't be a maid or cook hired by the landlady. No one living in the miserable district of Spitalfields could afford staff.

"I'm looking for Mrs. Metzger," Lincoln told her. "Or Miss Metzger. Is she here?"

The woman chewed on her bottom lip and hugged the door. "Who are you and what do you want?" she asked in a strong Russian accent.

"Is she here?" he asked again, trying to summon some patience. "It's urgent. Her life may be in danger."

She gasped and muttered a Russian expletive. "Why?" She didn't tell him he was too late, thankfully.

"Someone wants her dead. The reason is for her ears only. Please, fetch her for me."

"I am she."

He blew out a measured breath and placed his hands behind his back. "Someone is killing people with supernatural powers. I know that you're next on his list."

She covered another gasp with both hands, or rather, paws. Claws sprouted from her fingertips. When she realized, she shook them and the claws retracted. Her hands returned to normal. She pressed her lips together and glanced past him, left and right. She tucked her hands behind her back.

"I belong to an organization that protects your kind," he said. "I need to take you to safety. Now. Fetch whatever you can carry and come with me."

"But what about my work? My shift begin soon."

"Where do you work?"

"Gumm's Boots on Commercial."

"I'll tell them you were called away to an ill relative's bedside."

She continued to chew her lip.

"Your loved ones can come with you," he told her.

"I have no one. My husband and son dead."

He removed some money from his pocket. Her eyes widened. It was probably a year's worth of wages. "You can move out of London and rent a room for yourself. This should last you until you find work." He knew he was asking a lot of her, but if he couldn't save her...if she died because he hadn't alerted her yesterday...

He swallowed down the bile burning his throat. "I'll drive you to the station."

"I pack. Wait."

He retreated to the cabriolet. Another woman emerged from the house and paused when she spotted him. She was younger than Mrs. Metzger, but looked just as tired. She edged past him and hurried off along the street, her shoulders stooped.

Mrs. Metzger returned barely ten minutes later with a carpet bag that looked like it had traveled the world. Worn and stained, it nevertheless looked sturdy. Lincoln tied it to the back of the cabriolet.

"I will go to Southampton where there is sea and good air." Her face lifted and the sagging seemed not so pronounced. She held out her hand for the money and he passed it to her. She tucked it into her bodice then climbed up beside him.

"May I ask you a question about your hands?" he asked as the horse pulled away from the gutter.

She folded her gloved hands in her lap. "You may."

"Is that the only part of you that changes? Or is there something more to your magic?"

"Only my hands change, but I see the dead too."

"You're a medium? Or a necromancer?"

"What are these?"

"A medium speaks to the spirits of the recently deceased, but a necromancer can summon those long dead and bring them back to life."

She gasped then crossed herself. "I am medium. I see new spirits, before cross over."

He flicked the reins to drive the horse through the thickening morning traffic. They sat in silence, allowing Lincoln to think. Did the killer suspect Mrs. Metzger was a necromancer and had decided to eliminate her, just in case? Or was he now attacking supernaturals of any sort, no matter if they couldn't be used to reanimate the dead? If so, then everyone in the ministry archives was in danger.

A half hour later, he'd deposited Mrs. Metzger at Waterloo Station and headed home. She was safe, and perhaps she might even be happier living at the seaside than in London. He'd told her to contact him at Lichfield once she was settled. He would add her new location to the files, and keep those files locked away from untrustworthy eyes.

The house was quiet when he entered via the courtyard door, and he didn't need a seer's powers to know why. Gus and Seth were gone. He bypassed the kitchen but felt the venom of Cook's glare nevertheless. A resounding thump of the rolling pin left Lincoln in no doubt that Cook blamed him for his friends' departure.

Lincoln took the stairs two at a time, only to stop dead when he met Lady Vickers on the landing. She greeted him with a smile, which surprised him. Shouldn't she be upset about her son leaving? Shouldn't she be worried that Lincoln would throw her out now? The last time they'd spoken, she'd stoked Lincoln's temper and been determined that he should treat Seth as an equal, at the very least. So why the smile?

"Good morning, Mr. Fitzroy. I see you've been out already, and in such gloomy weather too."

"It has only just begun to rain." He stepped aside, but she didn't move to pass him.

A small crinkle appeared across her smooth brow. "You look troubled," she said, her smile fading.

"I've got some things on my mind now that your son and Gus have left my employ."

"Ah. I was wondering if you were going to bring it up or if I should."

"You are welcome to remain here, madam, whether Seth is present or not. I gave my word."

She squeezed his arm gently. Her eyes misted but quickly cleared and she resumed the mask of nobility again. It had to be a mask, he'd decided. This woman had run off with her footman, of all people. She *seemed* above such things, yet apparently she wasn't. Not that he was the best judge of character, particularly where Lady Vickers was concerned. He didn't understand her at all.

"You are a true gentleman, Mr. Fitzroy. Thank you. If Seth comes to me for advice, I will tell him in no uncertain terms that he must return here. He made an unwise decision, and I'm deeply troubled by it."

"But you don't want him to be my servant."

"No, I don't. But nor do I want him to have nothing, not even a roof over his head. He told me you pay him well, Mr. Fitzroy, and I am not so foolish as to think he's above working *with* you."

As opposed to *for* him. "Do you know where he is?" Lincoln asked.

"No, but I expect him to show his face sooner or later. I am his mother, after all. He can't run away from me too."

Seth wouldn't see it as running away. More like taking a stand. "Thank you, madam, but it's unnecessary. I won't force him to work for me." Coerce, yes, but not force.

He went to walk past her since she made no move to pass him, but she clung to his arm. "Did you go through the calling cards?"

"I haven't had time."

"You had many visitors, as did my Seth. You could both have the pick of the year's debutantes." Her eyes lit up with the same gleam he'd seen when she pushed Seth toward eligible women at the ball. Why was she looking at Lincoln like that? "If you want them, that is."

"I don't."

Her grip tightened. She wasn't letting him go yet. "Do you know why I came home to England, Mr. Fitzroy?"

"No." Nor did he want to know. Unfortunately it looked like she was going to keep her hand on his arm until she told him.

"I was lonely. My second husband died, and I'd made few friends in New York. Without friends to introduce me, I wasn't received into the right circles, you see. So I came home to be with my son again."

He nodded. Should he say something too?

"I loved him, you know," she said before he had a chance to think of an appropriate response. "My second husband was a good man, more of a gentleman than my first, even though *he* was the one born to gentility."

"You don't need to justify your actions to me. I don't care."

"Oh, I know that. That's why I like you so much."

She did? He couldn't tell.

"I expect I'll find myself shunned by English society for some time." She sighed. "There will be crude jokes and snide comments, of course, and I'll need to partner either Seth or your intriguing self if I wish to attend parties." Her strong features softened a little, but there was no other sign that she was bothered by these facts.

"Is there a reason you're telling me this?" he asked.

"I'm telling you because I want you to know that it was worth it. Even if I'd known George wasn't going to live long, and even if I'd known that returning to England would be difficult, I would still have married him."

Her face softened more and Lincoln grew worried that she would cry. He steeled himself. "I see," he said, glancing past her.

Instead of letting go, she held his arm tighter. "I don't think you do. You're trying to escape."

He cleared his throat and gave her his full attention.

Shouldn't she be saying these things to Seth? Why did she want to tell Lincoln these personal thoughts when she hardly knew him?

"I loved George very much," she said again. "Even though that love cost me a great deal, I couldn't have *not* loved him. I didn't have any choice in the matter. It simply was. Now do you see?"

He saw. He saw that Seth had told his mother more than he should have about Charlie. "I have to go."

She released his arm and he moved past her. "True love doesn't end," she said to his back. "It only deepens with time."

"Your advice is unwanted."

"My presence in London is unwanted by most, but I'm staying anyway. Love isn't always easy, Mr. Fitzroy, but nothing rewarding is."

She'd probably read that in one of the gothic romance novels he'd seen her reading.

It was too early for a drink and he didn't want to summon Doyle to fetch tea. While he didn't think the butler was the lecturing type, Lincoln would rather not risk it. He'd had enough advice and angry glares from the rest of the household to last a lifetime. Now he wanted peace to consider the developments in the investigation.

Unfortunately, a knock on the door disturbed him. It was only Doyle, delivering tea. Lincoln was beginning to wonder if the man had some supernatural seer powers after all. Or perhaps he was simply an excellent butler.

"Sir, I should warn you," Doyle said before exiting. "Cook is talking about leaving too."

Lincoln sat heavily in his chair. The task of replacing his staff suddenly felt overwhelming. He rubbed his forehead and listened to the door click closed as Doyle left. He sipped his tea and tried to think about work again. He should send someone to warn all of the London-based supernaturals to be vigilant, but there was no one left to send. Not even Cook. Lincoln expected him to march into his rooms with a meat cleaver at any moment. With his excellent aim and fierce temper, Cook would be a formidable opponent.

He set the teacup down and left. He slowed as he passed Charlie's rooms but forced himself to continue. *Anywhere but in there.* He headed up to the attic and the files stored there, but found himself detouring to the tower room. It stood empty and cold. The hearth had been swept clean and the mattress stripped bare. The last time he'd been in the room was the day Charlie left.

Charlie.

He shouldn't have come to the tower room. The memories of the day she left were too vivid here. But he didn't leave. He couldn't. He *wanted* to be there, to remind himself that he'd sent her away for bloody good reasons.

He sat on the windowsill and, for a moment, he couldn't remember those reasons. All he could see through the misty rain was the exact spot on the drive where the carriage had been when Charlie climbed into it that day.

She had cried. A lot. He'd almost given in and changed his mind, on numerous occasions, but somehow he'd stood firm. He'd focused on being calm, on shutting himself off, piece by piece. When he'd first learned the calming technique as a child, he'd thought of himself as a canal filled with dozens of locks. Each gated lock would close and shut off the water flow, leaving the downstream water level low. It wasn't until he was older and saw a working lock that he'd realized the gates reopened eventually. The technique still worked, however, and he'd perfected it over the years so that he could shut himself off and let nothing through. Not even Charlie's tears.

He'd stood in this same position and watched her raise her hand to the cab's rear window in either a wave or plea.

She'd seen him in that moment, watching her, and he'd stepped quickly out of her line of sight. But he'd still been able to see the coach, all the way to the front gate. He'd stayed in that room for hours afterward and stared out the window, just like he was now.

But there'd been no sickening feeling in his gut then, and no ache in his chest. No pounding in his head and certainly no regrets. He had done the right thing, and that mattered most. He *must* remember why he'd sent her to the School for Wayward Girls in the first place.

To keep her safe.

So he could focus on his work.

So she could have a normal future.

Damn his employees and Lady Vickers for making him doubt his decision. They were wrong to want Charlie back.

He lowered his hand from the pane. His palm left a mark on the frosty glass. He pushed off from the windowsill and strode out of the tower room. The house was too quiet. When he'd first arrived at Lichfield Towers, he'd wandered through the halls and rooms, lifting dust covers, checking the plans for the hidden nooks and corridors. He'd learned every inch of every wall, cupboard, and floorboard. It was a grander residence than General Eastbrooke's house and it was all his, according to the property documents. Yet it was nothing more than a pile of bricks and tiles. If it had burned down, he wouldn't have cared.

Until Charlie came. She'd filled it with her small frame and her big eyes, and a spirit that not even the walls could contain. Without her, Lichfield was just bricks and tiles again.

He strode on, unaware of his whereabouts until he found himself outside Charlie's door. It had been locked since her departure, the key kept in his desk drawer. Every time he'd opened the drawer it had reminded him of what he'd done. Sometimes he even remembered why he'd sent her away.

He dug the key from his pocket, having collected it the day before for a reason he could no longer recall. He pushed open her door and drew in a deep breath. Then another.

No one had been inside since Charlie left, not even Doyle. Ashes clogged the grate in the sitting room, and a book lay open on the table by the window. She'd forgotten to pack it. He placed the ribbon marker inside and closed it. He tucked it against his chest and, with another deep breath, headed through to her bedroom.

The dresser drawers stood open, and a few hairpins lay scattered atop the dressing table. All of her clothes were gone except for the boys' trousers and shirt she'd worn that first day she'd come to Lichfield. Everything had changed that day. In a way, he'd known it too. Instinct had told him that the scrawny lad with the lice-ridden hair and bad attitude would be an important part of his life from that day onward. He could never have fathomed in what manner, however. Not then. Even if he'd known she was a girl, he wouldn't have guessed that he would want to marry her within a few short months.

His gut twisted. Nausea rose to his throat. He sat on the unmade bed, suddenly dizzy. From the memories? The misery? No, that couldn't have caused this physical response.

He tried to shut it off, tried to close the lock gates, but no matter how hard he tried, he couldn't. The ability to shut himself off had vanished along with Charlie.

So he allowed the gates to swing wide open. Dizziness swamped him. The room spun around him, unbalancing him. He tilted to the side and fell onto the bed, his cheek on Charlie's pillow. He closed his eyes and reached for the seer's senses he usually kept in check.

He sat bolt upright. His heart pounded a single, loud thud

then stopped. He suddenly understood—the sickening feeling in his gut and the dizziness weren't from sadness or regret. They were caused by dread.

Charlie was in danger.

Lincoln had made a monumental mistake.

NOW AVAILABLE:
FROM THE ASHES
The 6th book in the Ministry of Curiosities series.

What will happen when Lincoln and Charlie meet again?

GET A FREE SHORT STORY

I wrote a short story featuring Lincoln Fitzroy that is set before THE LAST NECROMANCER. Titled STRANGE HORIZONS, it reveals how he learned where to look for Charlie during a visit to Paris. While the story can be read as a standalone, it contains spoilers from The 1st Freak House Trilogy, so I advise you to read that series first. The best part is, the short story is FREE, but only to my newsletter subscribers. So subscribe now via my website if you haven't already.

A MESSAGE FROM THE AUTHOR

I hope you enjoyed reading ASHES TO ASHES as much as I enjoyed writing it. As an independent author, getting the word out about my book is vital to its success, so if you liked this book please consider telling your friends and writing a review at the store where you purchased it. If you would like to be contacted when I release a new book, subscribe to my newsletter at http://cjarcher.com/contact-cj/newsletter/. You will only be contacted when I have a new book out.

ALSO BY C.J. ARCHER

SERIES WITH 2 OR MORE BOOKS

After The Rift

Glass and Steele

The Ministry of Curiosities Series

The Emily Chambers Spirit Medium Trilogy

The 1st Freak House Trilogy

The 2nd Freak House Trilogy

The 3rd Freak House Trilogy

The Assassins Guild Series

Lord Hawkesbury's Players Series

Witch Born

SINGLE TITLES NOT IN A SERIES

Courting His Countess

Surrender

Redemption

The Mercenary's Price

ABOUT THE AUTHOR

C.J. Archer has loved history and books for as long as she can remember and feels fortunate that she found a way to combine the two. She spent her early childhood in the dramatic beauty of outback Queensland, Australia, but now lives in suburban Melbourne with her husband, two children and a mischievous black & white cat named Coco.

Subscribe to C.J.'s newsletter through her website to be notified when she releases a new book, as well as get access to exclusive content and subscriber-only giveaways. Her website also contains up to date details on all her books: http://cjarcher.com She loves to hear from readers. You can contact her through email cj@cjarcher.com or follow her on social media to get the latest updates on her books:

facebook.com/CJArcherAuthorPage

twitter.com/cj_archer

instagram.com/authorcjarcher

pinterest.com/cjarcher

bookbub.com/authors/c-j-archer

Manufactured by Amazon.ca
Acheson, AB

11066210R00076